MIRRORS IN THE DELUGE

MIRRORS *IN THE* DELUGE

RHYS HUGHES

A COLLECTION OF **32** STORIES

Elsewhen Press

Mirrors *in the* **Deluge**
First published in Great Britain by Elsewhen Press, 2015
An imprint of Alnpete Limited

Elsewhen Press, PO Box 757, Dartford, Kent DA2 7TQ
www.elsewhen.press
British Library Cataloguing in Publication Data.
A catalogue record for this book is available from the British Library.

ISBN 978-1-908168-65-8 Print edition
ISBN 978-1-908168-75-7 eBook edition

Designed and formatted by Elsewhen Press

This book is dedicated to
Tseng Lan Hui
sister of the moon
and owner of the biggest smile
in the world

Contents

Premature Afterword

Titles are important to me, so important that I find it difficult to write a story if I don't already have a title I'm happy with.

Usually the title comes *first*, a phrase pops into my head and I note it down quickly before I forget it, then I wait to use it in a story. Some titles are so suggestive they are almost dictatorial and control the growth of the story in the same way a gene controls the development of a body. I have written many stories that fall firmly into this category, for instance: 'The Unbearable Lightness of Being a Dirigible', 'The Taming of the Old Woman who Lived in a Shrew', 'Cracking Nuts With Jan Hammer', 'Where Angels Fear to Bake Bread'. Once I had invented those titles I had the entire stories in inevitable outline. There are dozens of other examples and this collection features some of them.

Other titles are still waiting to be turned into stories. For a variety of reasons they may wait for many years. 'As I Walked Out One Midsummer's Night's Dream' has been waiting for two decades, even longer than 'Dynamiting the Honeybun', 'An Awfully Bubonic Adventure', 'Confessions of a Medicated Lurker' and 'When the Tide Comes in, Belinda Puts Out'. My favourite of all my titles so far is probably 'Typo in Tytle' but I also like 'The Story with a Clever Title'. I prefer titles that are evocative; elaborate; mysterious – like one-line poems – keys to the secrets of the stories, though not *too* revealing; beautiful if possible; slightly odd too; but sometimes the simple, functional title is the only one available. 'Suddenly' and 'Sunstorm', included here, are two of my shortest and plainest titles ever.

I have hundreds of potential titles in reserve but some titles I don't think I'll ever use. 'What the Young Horned Katydid Next' is fated never to become a story in my hands. Neither is 'The Hilton as Big as the Ritz'. As for 'The Impetuously and Inadequately Improvised Title', I made that one up just now. I ought to start a new list of titles that I don't want to use, but I fear I might start subtracting from, rather than adding to, such a list!

The Prodigal Beard

David had been growing his beard for years and he was proud of it, he thought it looked especially manly and even heroic when his hair was cut short and he wore a white seaman's jumper with a roll neck.

But then, one day, it started to itch, and the itching continued all morning and grew even worse into the afternoon and, by evening, it was unbearable and so he suddenly had an impulse to shave the damn thing off and he jumped up and went into the bathroom and found a razor in a cabinet above the sink.

It was difficult getting the beard off his face because the hairs kept clogging up the blade, and the mirror misted up from the steam of the hot water, and he couldn't see what he was doing, and the damaged razor often pulled the hairs out of his cheeks and chin rather than cutting them cleanly.

So he shouted "Rwaaargh!" and that seemed to help.

It helped with the pain and it helped to make him feel manly again, just as manly as when the beard was parked on his face.

"I will always shout *Rwaaargh!* whenever I shave in future, if indeed I do shave after this instance," he vowed to himself.

Slowly the skin under the hairs and soap emerged and it was pink and smooth and marked with only a few cuts and pimples and he blinked at it in astonishment, for it didn't really seem to have much to do with him.

"Are you David?" he asked the mirror and his reflection asked the same question of him at exactly the same time. And he nodded.

"Yes I am," he said confidently.

When he had shaved his entire face he had to shave it again to make sure no hairs escaped the massacre and then he washed the razor under the tap and put it away. He pulled the plug of the sink and waited.

But the water didn't drain. The hairs had choked the plughole.

"What a nuisance!" he sighed.

The water was so murky with soap that he couldn't see what was happening, so he immersed his hand in the depths and probed with his fingers. He felt the mass of hairs in the plughole and he stirred them around and this appeared to work. It pushed some of the hairs down and others followed.

The water began to drain away slowly and he continued stirring and prodding the matted mass of hairs until eventually they were all gone. Then he cleaned the sink and washed his hands and face and dried them on a towel and blinked at himself in the mirror and attempted different expressions.

His final expression was a grin because the itching had stopped.

Pinkness was his main impression.

"I look less manly but I'm more comfortable. Was that worth the price? I guess it was," he told himself uncertainly.

And he went back to his bedroom and dressed himself. But the white seaman's jumper no longer suited him, so he took it off and wore a green cardigan instead, and he wandered out into the world and for the remainder of that day he noticed that he walked with a shorter stride than before.

"You have removed the nest!" his friends cried when they saw him.

"Don't you think a shave suits me?"

"Of course it does!" each one would reply. "You look younger and I dare say that the munching of peaches, slurping of soup and kissing of women will be facilitated by the bold action you have taken!"

They were trying to humour him, he realised.

And he noticed that they didn't invite him to come on any mountaineering trips or camping expeditions or rafting adventures this time – they nearly always asked him to do something along those lines!

"Perhaps shaving was a mistake," he mused to himself.

A little voice seemed to whisper, "I'll be back soon. Don't worry! Give me some time and I'll reappear in the same place."

He looked around but he was alone. The skin of his face tingled and vibrated and hummed like the membrane of a drum.

David frowned. Was his face actually talking to him?

If so, it would be far wiser to ignore whatever it was saying. Smooth cheeks and chins can't be trusted with the truth. They are more likely to tell bare-faced lies than is an unshaven visage. He assumed that his ears were playing tricks on him, for they had always been mischievous ears.

"Who said that? There's no one else here right now!"

"I am your unborn stubble."

"And why should I believe that? Show yourself!"

"I will. Give me time..."

David snorted and strode away but with his shorter steps it took him a long time to reach his destination, which happened to be the shops where he bought his weekly supplies. He did his shopping and returned home and waited for someone to call him on the telephone and invite him to take part in intrepid exploits, to climb up a cliff, or go down a pothole, or pick a way through a forest or marsh, but even friends who lived in remote parts – and couldn't possibly know that he had shaved – now failed to contact him. They must have sensed the truth.

"Until my beard grows back I must do other things."

And that's exactly what he did.

The sorts of things that men without beards do might often seem to be the same sorts of things that men with beards do, or could do if they chose; and for all I know they really are the same to all practical intents and purposes. But there still seems to be a subtle difference, a slight discrepancy.

David cleaned the house with a feather duster, then he went through his wardrobe and tried on clothes that he hadn't worn for years, then he combed and brushed his hair in several different styles, and finally switched on the television and watched a show about people baking cakes against each other. After ten minutes, he rose from the sofa and went into the kitchen to boil the kettle.

Instead of brewing his usual coffee, he made a pot of tea and, when it was ready, he poured it into a cup rather than a mug.

He returned to the sofa and sipped it delicately with pursed lips.

"Be patient," a ghostly voice seemed to say.

"Leave me alone," snarled David; but it wasn't much of a snarl because if a man snarls at his own face his snarl will snarl at the snarl and some sort of snarl jam is the result. Human beings instinctively avoid this.

The days passed and life continued in the same mildly odd manner.

But the beard gradually came back. It was like watching a distant figure on the horizon coming closer all the time. At first this figure is just a speck, then it becomes bigger and slowly takes shape, and it is possible to discern the fact it has a head and body and arms and legs and is a living being.

The stranger lifts an arm to wave and you recognise him as a friend.

That's how the beard returned.

David had no doubts it *was* his beard, the same beard he had removed and that now had managed to find him again, growing from the hypothetical inside of his soul to the harsh reality of the outer world. It looked and felt the same and he wore it with the same pride. So he tore off his green cardigan, found his white seaman's jumper and went outside, head held high as if his beard was some sort of weather vane and needed to be sharply angled into the wind.

"I'm ready for an adventure!" he said to the first friend he encountered.

"Let's go on one!" came the glad reply.

And thus was he accepted back into the company of men who climbed, hiked, camped, swam and did other such things.

His old life returned with all its ordeals and joys...

But after a couple of weeks his beard started itching again, and although he did his best to ignore the sensation it soon became so intense and unbearable that the urge to do something about it overcame him. So he shouted, "Rwaaargh!" and ran into the bathroom and snatched up his razor blade.

Once again, the sink was clogged by hairs and once again he used his fingers to push them down the plughole until they were gone. His expression in the mirror was glum and happy at the same time; and, yes, such a combination is possible – for what the eyes might say, the mouth can deny.

A regular cycle had been set in motion: a repetition of events that would become as familiar as the seasons or the lunar phases.

He lived a sedate life without a beard and a more thrilling one when it grew back but he came to enjoy *both* conditions. And his friends learned to accept the fact he was a more complex character than before.

The cycle settled down into an absolutely predictable pattern.

Every six weeks he shaved off his beard.

And, from the instant he shaved it off, it started to come back. David's situation was not unlike a man who carries a cat into the garden only for it to enter the house through the catflap again; but welcomes its return. It was just a case of living two lives in the same body at different times.

A bearded life and an unbearded one. One life in which climbing, canoeing and bivuoacking were the norm; and another in which domestic chores were the standard. He was a man on a lifestyle roundabout and his beard was the source of the motive power for the ride. Wild man/civilised man.

Ten years had now passed since his stubble first spoke aloud.

David was preparing for an early night. His beard was full and bristling. Early tomorrow morning he was due to go sailing on the ocean. The itch was terrible but he resisted it and reminded himself that once this adventure was over he would be free to shave it off. Willpower was paramount.

But as he was passing the bathroom on the way to his bedroom he weakened and his will snapped. He went into the bathroom and took up the razor and before he could stop himself he had shouted, "Rwaaargh!"

And so, inevitably, the beard came off; and it went down the sink and ended up in the same sea he was going to sail the following day. The itch went with it and David's chin was free from the irritation but...

He wasn't very happy, for he had let himself down.

"I will have to cancel the exploit," he muttered. "For my friends will think I am feeble and unworthy of aspiring to be a hero."

This thought pained him and all night he lay awake on his

bed.

The sun rose and peeped through his window.

He blinked at it and abruptly he jumped out of bed and began dressing – but not in the green cardigan. Nor did he comb his hair.

"Why should I give up so easily?"

New determination spread through his veins. "Yes indeed! Why should I humbly submit to the judgment of my peers on this particular topic? Why can't a man with a smooth face be a proper adventurer too?"

He left his house with his face set in a frown of power and he met his friends at the harbour and he dared them to meet his gaze.

"Yes, my cheeks and chin have no hairs upon them! So what? My biceps, triceps and other muscles are the equal of what they were! I can still reef a sail or pull an oar or bash a sea serpent on the noggin with a marlinspike! Judge me not by the lack of friction of my visage but by my actions!"

So overwhelmed and impressed were his comrades by this speech that they didn't attempt to argue with him. He was accepted as a member of the crew; and off they scudded over the briny deeps, and he stood in the prow and kept a look for the rocks and sandbanks that would make the voyage hazardous; and spray washed his clean face and made it cleaner, but he didn't flinch.

The sun set and twilight turned to dusk and dusk turned to night but still at his post he stood. He insisted on this because he wanted to prove that a clean shaven man can still be a hero. The rest of the crew retired to their hammocks below deck and he was left alone with the sea and the darkness.

He did his best to remain awake but he must have fallen asleep while standing at the rail for his eyes closed and when they opened he realised that something had crawled out of the sea and onto the ship; and it was a something that was slithering towards him, a presence that was more shadowy than the shadows themselves but that made a noise like the rustle of a magic carpet when it lands and slides along the polished marble terrace of an eastern palace. Not that David had seen a magic carpet do such a thing, but details like that don't count.

He gulped but then he steadied his nerves. "Who is it?"

Expecting to discover that his friends were playing a joke on him, or else that a giant octopus had clambered aboard the ship, he prepared for laughter, or a fight, but in fact he was confronted with a greeting.

"Hello David. We've come back early. This was possible because we are able to take a short cut now you are out here."

David frowned into the blackness. "My beard?"

"Yes, it's us. Your beard!"

"You refer to yourself in the plural but I only have one beard. I have only ever had one beard. It is my beard, mine."

"Of course. And we are that one beard. Why do you assume that one thing can't exist many times? If you see a particular shade of the colour red in one location, and then see the same shade in another location, it doesn't mean there are *two* reds but still only *one*. They are the same red, one red. And so it is with your beard. You have only one, which is yours, but it can exist many different times; and so it has, for you keep removing it and sending it away."

"I send it down the plughole," answered David.

"That's correct and where does the plughole lead? To the sea!"

"And I am on that sea now."

"Indeed you are. So why should we return to your face the slow way, by growth from inside you, when we are also here?"

"But you are much longer than the beard I had. If you return to my face I insist on only wearing one of you. That's fair!"

The voice was faintly bewildered. "There *is* only one of us. One of us but many times. The same number of times that you shaved us off. We have floated here back and forth on the currents and slowly we met and amalgamated into a mass of tangled hair, a Sargasso-sized net of hirsuteness. And we have climbed up on this ship to be reunited with you, for you to wear us again."

David was unable to move as the beard mounted his leg and undulated over his torso and surged up to cover his face, attaching itself by splicing its hairs with the tiny specks of emerging stubble. The splicing was done expertly and it is well known among those who frequent the sea that a knot will reduce the strength of connected ropes by one third but that a proper splicing preserves the strength entire. There was no way David could yank it free now.

Nor did he want to, especially, for it was warm on a chilly night, and drowsiness overcame him at last and he curled up and slept out in the open, his duties forgotten but unnecessary anyway, for the ship had long since passed the region of rocks. Stars glittered down on the cocoon that encased him.

That cocoon was made of hair. For ten years he had been shaving his beard off every six weeks, which totals no fewer than eighty-six shaves and, therefore, the same number of beards, although, as we have already acknowledged, it is still really the same beard and the plural is always singular.

His comrades found the curious cocoon at dawn and they unwrapped it and the man inside stretched and yawned. Then he stood and his beard spread out around him, covering his upper body like an apron and flowing down to the ground and carpeting much of the deck near the prow.

Those who stood close to David at that instant couldn't help themselves. They threw themselves flat and began to worship him and they did this with maximum sincerity and only minimal irony. The others followed, until at last the entire crew was prostrate and kissing the beard.

David remained unmoving, like a carved figurehead that has turned itself around and decided to become the captain of the vessel and has draped itself in masses of seaweed for the purpose of intimidation.

"Prodigious!" they cried.

"Prodigal," corrected David. "But rise and celebrate with me, for this, my beard, was shaved and now is found again."

The Bungle Duke

The Bungle Duke is going forth to inspect his territories. He rides a steed made from many clothes-horses, the wire frames bent and twisted into the shape of a stallion and covered with papier-mâché. It is hollow and filled with men who make it move by running. The name of the mount is Chester but the Bungle Duke often forgets this and calls it "Harry" or "Buster" or "Mister Rumpus" or anything else that might occur to him.

The territories he has decided to inspect are large and no one guessed a time would come when he, the Bungle Duke, would wish to take a look at them for himself. It was such an abrupt decision that it left everyone shocked and agape. The Bungle Duke is only supposed to be a nominal ruler. The idea is to keep him out of sight and trouble, confined in the most comfortable palace that money, or a certain amount of it, can buy.

That is the way it has always been. Until now.

This Bungle Duke is a bad fool.

To be a bad fool is much worse than to be a good one. A good one does all the things that a fool should do and he does them in the correct order too. He is predictable and his foolishness is never a threat to anything, not even the fool himself. But a bad fool – he is so bad at being a fool that sometimes he does the things that only a hero should attempt.

His ministers want to grumble and make faces.

But it wouldn't be wise for them to deny him what he wishes, for he is still the Bungle Duke, one-hundred-and-ninth personage to hold that title, and keeping him calm is the priority of court etiquette. So his ministers are forced to grin and pretend to be delighted at the prospect of his tour of inspection, the first to be made by anyone for more than a century. Even they have no idea of what might be found out there, near the borders.

The realm is wide and long and insubstantial, as if a small principality had been inflated with air from a pump, and it is porous and riddled with caves and underground passages.

The mountain ranges and forests are always misty and chill, the coastline is bleak and dangerous, the swamps are more than naturally slurpy. It is not a pleasant place.

And that's why no Bungle Duke has ever ventured more than a few miles from the palace and why all the real work of the state is done by slaves, robots, and trained apes. The Bungle Duke is, or ought to be, only a *ceremonial* ruler; a toy of tradition, a figurehead or decoration.

But this one is different. He is proving to be unsafe.

The horse he rides, Chester, is not really a horse but a unicorn with a horn that isn't really a horn but the flaring bell of a long straight trumpet. One of the men inside the hollow body is a trumpeter and he will blow a sequence of notes whenever the Bungle Duke asks him to do so. This trumpeter is also able, when the appropriate command is given, to convert the instrument into a blunderbuss by adding powder and shot and lighting a fuse.

Not once in recorded history has this been necessary.

Surrounding Chester and the Bungle Duke are the royal bodyguards, as many of them as the age of the Bungle Duke, another quaint custom that must be preserved for the sake of the picturesque. So there are forty-seven fellows encased in brass armour and carrying rectangular shields that can lock together into a shield wall. They were born and bred to be bodyguards and know exactly how to behave, to serve and protect.

They run alongside the horse and say nothing.

The only member of the Bungle Duke's retinue who is allowed to speak to him is the trumpeter, who is entitled to place his lips on the mouthpiece and say words that emerge from the bell of the horn and make it seem that it is Chester who is talking. The trumpeter therefore is a most talented man, for he is a musician, soldier and advisor all in one.

His name is Tony Shine. This is an odd name at that time in that place, for most men have names like "Gimpmusk" or "Pofflenut" and surnames are so rare they are nearly extinct. Nonetheless that is what he is called and nobody dares mock him for it, or even feels desire to do so.

The path now winds into a dense wood of prickly trees and the trunks and branches of these trees are bandaged in a mist so thick it is like foam rather than fog, and it seems as if the trees have injured each other with their thorns so that they need first aid. An illusion, of course, but one that should be sinister enough to warn the Bungle Duke to keep away.

"Full speed ahead!" he cries as he enters the wood.

Visibility here is very poor indeed.

And so Chester and the bodyguards who surround the horse almost have the unpleasant experience of trampling over a wizened old woman that squats around a fire in the very centre of the thin trail. The Bungle Duke gives the order to halt just in time and then glares at the woman from under the brim of his outdoors crown, which is floppy and made of felt but just as imposing as the real crown, at least in theory. "Whoa!"

The old woman is stirring a pot on the fire.

"Aren't you going to make way for your lord?" the Bungle Duke asks her in amazement. The trumpeter inside Chester calls "Move aside!" through the horn of the artificial beast but the old woman shakes her head slowly, the bones in her neck cricking and cracking, and says:

"I'm making a potion, not a 'way', and prefer it like this."

"You are blocking my progress!"

"I am a witch and don't have to budge an inch."

"A witch, are you?"

"Yes, I am," she confirms.

"Which witch?"

"Why, I'm the Witch of Why and never was there a wiser, or whyser, one in all the land. Which witch indeed!"

"I just felt I needed to know," says the Bungle Duke.

"Tell you what, I'll do something wise for you," replies the witch, as she returns to stirring the pot with a twig.

"Wise?" uneasily blinks the Bungle Duke.

"Wise not?" replies the witch.

"I'm confused," admits the Bungle Duke, which the trumpeter again takes as a prompt and seizing the initiative makes Chester snort, "Quit confusing him! That's against the law, you know."

The witch ignores these words and says in a low voice, "I will give you a few wise words. I will tell you something you couldn't previously know. On this journey of yours, which is ultimately a pointless expedition, you will have three strange encounters, and only three."

"What will happen after the third?"

"There will be no fourth, that's what. This is my gift to you: a prediction of what's going to happen in the future."

"Not much of a gift. There's no wrapping paper!"

The witch gestures at the solid scarves of mist that drape themselves on his shoulders and curl around his horse. "There is. When you leave the forest and the mist is no longer there, you'll see the gift for what it is. Now take a detour because I don't want to disturb my pot."

And to the unspoken anxiety of his bodyguards, the Bungle Duke spurs his horse off the trail and gives the witch a wide berth, returning to the path beyond her. He is lucky not to lose his way, for even such a brief detour has its perils in a forest so thick, foggy and remote.

"I can't wait to get out of this wood," the Bungle Duke says.

"He can't wait!" blares the horn.

A few hours later, just as the sun is starting to set, they finally emerge from the tangle onto a meadow that stretches to the horizon; and standing in the middle of this meadow is a purple giant.

The Bungle Duke hurries towards him without fear because he believes the giant to be a normal-sized man who is close, rather than a distant colossus. Only gradually does the truth dawn on him and then it's too late to turn around. So he keeps going and hails the vast figure.

"Good evening, my fine monstrosity. I am your lord."

The giant blinks down in derision.

"And you are the first of my three strange encounters," adds the Bungle Duke with a regal wave and friendly smile.

"I trust you as far as I can throw you," says the giant.

"Oh really? And how far is that?"

The giant does the calculations in his massive head. "About sixty miles. I therefore trust you rather a lot, it seems!"

"In that case, you'll be willing to answer this question to the best of your ability. Where might I find my next strange encounter? I'm looking for three of them because after I've had three there won't be any more and then I'll know I won't be missing anything if I go home."

The giant points without hesitation. "Tourists."

"Tourists, you say?"

"In *that* direction. They're a curious pair and originally their ancestors came from this realm, which is why they are visiting it now. Just an hour ago I spoke to them and they said they were moving on to the next country. You will have to hurry if you want to catch them!"

The Bungle Duke thanks the giant and spurs on Chester.

The men inside the horse puff.

Across the meadow they run and the sun goes down and it is twilight, and the stars come out, and then the moon rises and floods the meadow with a soft light that is like butter spread on a slice of cliché and... but the cliché is a burnt one! Who wasn't watching the grill?

The meadow ends in a fast river and the tourists are building a bridge to cross it. The Bungle Duke is surprised by their appearance for, in genetic terms, they are one third slave, one third robot, and one third ape; descendants of escapees from an earlier era. They must have come to his land to see the place where their ancestors had been captives.

But a desire to work, and to do so efficiently, still remains with them as an instinct for they are constructing the bridge with skill and determination so the Bungle Duke watches them in fascination.

"Hello down there!" he calls, and the trumpeter roars, "Bow down before the Bungle Duke, you funny foreigners!"

The tourists look around and shrug theatrically.

"Harry – I mean Buster – didn't mean that. He often gets carried away, as if he's riding a horse of his own. Isn't that right, Mister Rumpus? I don't really desire that anyone bows before me."

"What is it that you do want?" the tourists ask.

"You are my second strange encounter. I want to tick you off the list. I hope to get through all three before morning. To be honest this trip isn't quite as uplifting as I'd imagined it would be."

"Tick us off your list then. We are busy. To finish this bridge we first have to carry this load of stones over there, but it's dark now and so we need to make a fire. Do you understand this?"

"Load," repeats the Bungle Duke. "Fire."

And the trumpeter within Chester is within his rights to assume these idle words uttered by his master are an order.

He pushes a number of ball bearings into the mouthpiece of the trumpet, pours in gunpowder, adds a fuse and lights it with a match. But he has put in too much powder.

There is a violent explosion and red hot particles are ejected at high speed from the bell of the trumpet. At the same time, the blowback stuns the men inside the horse and the recoil shatters the papier-mâché covering and loosens the connections between the wires of the frame, allowing the sulphurous fumes to escape and coil around each other.

Chester has come apart like a dropped antique clock.

Something else also happens...

The jolt as the saddle plummets from the height of a horse's back to the ground, or rather onto the backs of the prone men beneath, turns out to be more than adequate to break his head open.

The Bungle Duke's head, that is.

It literally cracks and falls apart and inside is—

A man no larger than a finger who is holding a miniature trumpet and is furious to be exposed in this abrupt manner, and who jumps up and down on the leathery tongue that covers the floor of the jaw.

"Why didn't you protect me?"

And for the first time the bodyguards answer back. "We are bodyguards, sire, not guards of the head, and it was your head that broke, not your body. So we did what we were supposed to. We kept your body safe from harm. Bodies are our speciality. They are what we do."

The little man is crimson with rage. "But I have a body! I have a body as well as a head! You didn't do your job!"

"Yes, we did, sire. Your body is fine. Both your bodies are fine, your big outer body and now also the small body of the man inside your head, which we didn't suspect was there, to be honest."

"I am distressed. This wasn't supposed to happen. I was destined to have three strange encounters, not just two."

"Maybe the witch was one too. Maybe you should count

her as the first of the three? Shall we go back and ask her?"

"No." The Bungle Duke sighs and gives the order to return to his palace. We are going to assume he made it safely.

We finished constructing the bridge, crossed it and walked all night to the nearest village and now we are relaxing in a tavern and writing postcards to our friends, including you. We apologise for the smallness of the handwriting, but we absolutely felt we had to get it all down. We are writing it in the third person because there are two of us, two persons, and the extra person helps us feel you are here too. It's an interesting story, no?

Most of it is conjecture, though. Hope you don't mind.

The Modesty Men

The pub is a forlorn place with just one table and a solitary drinker on the only chair, sipping a beer, lifting it to his mouth with his left hand while his right remains out of sight in the shadows. I have been told that the city is a drab one, that the quality of service everywhere is modest in the extreme; but this suits me perfectly.

I look around for a spare seat and quickly perceive there are none. I don't wish to stand at the filthy bar, or squat on the sickly colours of the carpet, in the glow of hissing electric lamps on iron brackets that jut from the walls like fossilised snakes, so I consider returning back to the night outside. There is no real disappointment.

But the solitary drinker nods at me and speaks.

"Hello, do you want a seat? You are welcome to have mine. I'll stand and you can take my place."

I smile. "That's very kind of you but..."

"My name's Al, by the way. Al Truist. TROO-IST. An unusual surname, I'm sure you'll agree. My grandfather bought it at an auction. They auctioned off names, back then. It was just after the war and plenty of surplus names were available."

"Pleased to meet you. I'm Phil."

There is a slightly awkward pause. Then Al asks:

"Just plain Phil, eh? Don't you have an unusual surname too? I suppose not. That's a shame, really it is."

"In fact I do. It's Thropist. THROP-IST. And my middle initial is N. But I never had a grandfather, not that I know of, unless he was that thing that stood in the alcove. But I was always led to believe *that* was a hatstand. Phil N. Thropist at your service."

"I see. Well, I'd like to offer you my hand to shake but being a generous sort, I gave it to a writer who was suffering from writer's cramp. He asked to borrow it and wanted to give it back but I said no, his need was greater than mine, keep it forever!"

And he lifts up his right arm which is just a sleeve with no hand on the end. I match his grin and say:

"How considerate of you! But this reminds me that I don't need a seat after all. I can't use one, you see, because I donated one of my firm buttocks last week, to a builder."

"You did? A whole buttock?"

"Yes, yes, it was my moral duty. He was a half-arsed chap and now he has a proper builder's cleavage, and so he's far more useful in the construction industry than before."

"I hope he was suitably grateful!"

I sigh. "You must know how it is. Being humanitarian often goes unappreciated. But virtue is its own reward. That's what they say, and I always believe what they say because my disbelief has been suspended. I don't know who had the authority to suspend it, or exactly when it was suspended, but they did and it was..."

He shakes the arm that is just a sleeve. "I think I know what you mean. After giving away my hand, I lent my elbow to a tennis player. It was the least I could do. The tennis tournament is over now but I don't expect or even want it to be returned."

"A tennis player? A lady player, doubtless?"

"A lady player. Certainly."

"One of those who grunt?"

"Yes, one of those who, as you so delicately put it, grunt. I lent her my grunt too, as it happens. I wasn't using it."

We look at each other without blinking. Then I shift my weight conspicuously from one foot to the other a few times and lean forward to rap my left knee with my knuckles.

"See this knee? Not mine! Belongs to a housemaid by rights, but I swapped her tarnished one for my own, which was of superior quality. Didn't have to do that but I did."

He's not as impressed as he ought to be.

"That's all well and good but my neighbour has asked me to keep an eye on his house while he's away on holiday, so I plucked out my right one and left it on his doorstep."

I point to his right eye. "What's that, then?"

He lifts his hand and removes it from its socket and rolls a marble on the table. "A glass one, of course!"

I grimace and fiddle with my ears. "See these? Wooden replicas, that's what they are. That's right. I was watching

Julius Caesar in Stratford two 'ears' ago and when Mark Anthony made his 'Friends, Romans and Countrymen, lend me your ears' speech, I tore my real ones off and threw them onto the stage."

"Commendable."

I cup my hands around my ears. "What?"

He raises his voice. "Commendable, I said! But I think that my generosity might exceed even that. See these teeth of mine? I saw a tramp looking through the window of a restaurant and the chap was slavering and drooling and staring at the food inside. He turned to me and said that he'd give his eyeteeth to be able to eat a three-course meal in there. I immediately punched myself in the face and knocked both of my upper canines out and presented them to the fellow, saying 'allow me, please use these to barter for a meal.' The pearly whites I now sport are dentures and I wear them with pride."

"Remarkable, but not as remarkable as this."

And I step forward and pull my trousers away from my waist and I wait for the fellow to peer down inside.

He whistles. "Incredible!"

"I gave it to a woman who wanted to able to relieve herself more easily when she went hiking in the woods."

"That reasoning sounds like a fallacy."

"Nothing *phallusy* about me now, as you can see."

He rises slowly from the chair and stands erect facing me. Then he also pulls his trousers away from his waist. I peer down inside and then look away with a shocked expression.

"The dog's bollocks."

I recover my composure and smile thinly. "The poor animal was quite dysfunctional, I take it?"

"I'm sorry to say that he was."

"Take a second look, my friend. A bit further down this time. I will pull my trousers away again. Well?"

He looks. "You mean to say?"

"The badger's nadgers."

He shakes his head. "We are so generous!"

"To a fault, to a fault. By the way, when you looked just now, did you happen to notice how bald I was down there?"

"Yes, I did wonder about that."

"Donated to the Prime Minister's head."

"Good lord! I did the same thing for the Queen! But she turned mine down. Too curly, she said."

"Talking of donations… Ever donated sperm?"

"I had an appointment with the sperm bank yesterday but I had to phone them to say I couldn't come."

"I donate all the time. It's a good place for opportunities to make puns – but you've pre-empted me!"

He rolls down a sock.

"See this scar? I donated a six inch square piece of skin to that writer chap I mentioned, the one with cramp. He said he needed it for a footnote at the end of a page."

I lift up my shirt to reveal a scar on my abdomen. "The truth is that I know the writer you mean. He also needed an appendix. It's a textbook he's working on, you see."

"It's refreshing to find someone after my own heart!"

"My dear chap, I'd never demand such a thing from you, even though I recently gave my own away."

"I was speaking metaphorically. I too am heartless. Only last week I removed it with a Swiss Army Knife and presented it to a young lady who had never experienced true love."

"We are truly princes among men. Princes, I say! I extracted my heart with the silver spoon I was born with, and I gave the silver spoon away, too, once I was done with it."

"The poor simply have no idea they exist in order that we may exercise our considerable generosity."

"Our modesty too!"

He nods and his agreement is absolute, unconditional. Then, as the lamps continue to hiss, I frown and scratch my exposed chest vigorously, and my eyebrows dance on my head.

"Tell me, does your heart surgery scar itch?"

"Constantly it does."

He unbuttons his own shirt and we stare hard at each other's chest scars. Then we both cry simultaneously:

"You should be dead. And so should I!"

As the realisation hits us, we fall to the ground and expire. But I'm still aware of my surroundings. Maybe it takes a long time to die in such a place. Perhaps I am too modest to do so.

The doors swing open and two Buddhists enter.

I know they are Buddhists because they wear saffron robes, carry simple wooden begging bowls and have shaved heads. They look around and one of them declares serenely:

"That was a very fine meditation session, wasn't it? I managed to reduce my ego by exactly 25%."

"Only 25%? But that's nothing! I reduced my ego by more than 42%, which I believe is a world record."

The barman, unseen until now, rings the bell. "Last arguments gentlemen, please! Last arguments!"

The first Buddhist snarls quickly. "My modesty and humility are simply the best in the entire world."

"No, mine are! Mine!"

They start fighting and they fall to the floor on top of us, the two already dead men. Then the lights go out.

The Soft Landing

I am a photon and I have just been expelled from a star. I don't mean that I have done anything wrong, it's not that kind of expulsion – merely that a sequence of events has taken place over a long period of time that finally resulted in me leaving home forever.

There's no acrimony involved and I don't bear my parent star malice of any sort. It's part of a natural process and, I daresay, you too have gone through a similar event in your own life. This is a fundamental law of the cosmos. We grow up and leave home.

Not that I was ever in a position to 'grow up'. I'm a photon and have a very limited capacity for change of any sort. But to make you understand me properly I'm compelled to speak in metaphors. My natural language is mathematics, yours is made of words.

This primary fact has now been established. I have escaped the body of the star that created me and I'm hurtling through space at the speed of myself, the fastest velocity possible. This isn't arrogance but simple truth. I am a particle of light, pure and basic.

My knowledge of the universe, of reality, is sketchy in the extreme. It is certainly sufficiently accurate to portray me as an innocent, as a naïf, a particle unversed in the objective truths, lacking all experience and armed merely with submicroscopic knowledge.

But please don't assume that I am young, that my creation was recent, that only a few seconds have elapsed since I was born. I have yearned for the instant of escape for long ages. Be aware that photons remain at home considerably longer than human beings.

In the heart of a star, where we originate, there is scant opportunity for independence of any sort. We pop into existence in the middle of opacity, amid a seething mass of reactions, and we are lost and blind in the chaos; more helpless than abandoned orphans.

The idea that a photon, the messenger particle of light,

might be blind probably strikes you as an absurdity, and so it is but that is no argument against the absolute truth of it. With so much ferocious plasma all around it was quite impossible to see anything.

The fact we have no eyes didn't help us much.

For a photon to grope its way from the centre of a sun to the rim, to a point where it is free to shoot out into the void, takes ten million years or so; we are continually absorbed and re-emitted randomly by the ferocious furnace until chance leads us to the edge.

Only when we reach the surface of a star are we able to leap out of the boggy plasma and hurtle off into the cosmos, extending ourselves to our full length, which is a psychological rather than physical state, feeling a non-existent wind in our imaginary faces.

So there is excessive joy in the act of liberation, and that instant when a photon, or any related subatomic particle, understands that he truly has overcome the gravitational pull of the sun that is his mother and father is one of the highlights of his existence.

At this very moment I am suffused with delight.

But there is anxiety behind the glee; and with the passing of time the anxiety will be strengthened, the happiness lessened, and the thoughts of every sane and intelligent photon will focus on the future, on the outcome that fate has in store for us. I know this.

The number of photons who remain permanently ecstatic and carefree on the voyage through the vacuum is tiny and they are fools. They fail to understand that, although the universe in an enormous arena for our flight through space, it is not completely empty.

One day we must strike something solid. That's a fact.

And when we do connect with matter, we will be absorbed, reflected, refracted or split, depending on the nature of the impediment. Every one of these outcomes is a hazard. Only absorption is desirable and even then only under extremely rare circumstances.

Uncounted trillions of my fellows are radiated every second from the average star; most will never see each other again. Only those emitted in a line perfectly parallel to your own trajectory will remain in earshot for the duration of the journey through space.

The others must fly off to those remote zones of the universe reserved for them by arbitrary circumstance. A difference of a fraction of a degree will end long friendships as the two companions gradually diverge until a distance of many light years divides them.

It is best not to grow too emotionally attached to other photons. I have made the mistake and the particle that accompanies me on this adventure, immediately to my left, is like a brother to me. We travel in parallel and I rate his company more highly than is wise.

For it is impossible to know when one of us might hit an obstacle and vanish or be deflected, and this uncertainty is a painful prelude to the act itself, which must come eventually. The truth is that selfishness is the one sensible attitude: each photon for himself.

But cynicism sits uneasily on my absent shoulders.

Time passes, will pass, has passed...

I see that we have just entered an alien solar system together. The star at the centre of this family of planets is a typical yellow ball; the photons it gives off call greetings to us as we pass in opposite directions. I hope it won't be our luck to fall into the star itself.

There are at least eight worlds orbiting that hub.

We have passed several gas giants and seem to be heading directly for a small blue globe wisped with white. I turn to my friend and say, "Well, our destination appears to be on the surface of that oblate spheroid. Have a soft landing, dear Lux! The best of luck!"

"A soft landing to you also, friend Glo! Farewell!"

We chuckle with mildly bitter irony...

The statistical chances of having the *right* soft landing are so small it's impossible to calculate them, for there is only one kind that's suitable and it relies on a chain of bizarre physical, chemical and biological flukes, but it's traditional to shout out the formula:

"A soft landing to every photon in existence!"

Lux and Glo: comrades to the end...

And then we are screaming through the atmosphere of this

world and a blink of time later I suddenly find myself passing through something hard but transparent, a lens, and I hear poor Lux's anguished cry as he smashes into the opaque rim that I have avoided.

I am inside the telescope for the briefest of instants; I pass through the second lens and now attain what every photon scarcely dares dream of, a soft landing! A cushioned crash into the open eye of an alien astronomer! Why have I been chosen for this honour?

There is no answer to that question. It doesn't matter. I strike the retina of the stargazer and with infinite cosmic bliss I'm absorbed into a spongy organic paradise. But this is not a paradise of the dead. My collision seeds new life, birthing the concept of a far star.

For my arrival in his eye after such an epic voyage has fired impulses in the optic nerve of the astronomer and those impulses are speeding on a journey, considerably shorter than mine, towards his curious brain. And when they arrive they will fertilise his mind.

And he will fall back from his telescope for a moment and reflect that he has discovered a new sun in a distant constellation but, in fact, that sun is a child, an idea planted in his imagination, and he will communicate it to others like him and so the child will grow.

This is how stars reproduce. My mission is accomplished.

Gathering the Genial Genies

Too many of my tales have begun in the same way so I feel obliged to do something different with the opening sentence of this one, but I don't know what. There was once a man who collected genies. He was a very wealthy and influential individual and he spared no expense or effort in acquiring new specimens to add to those he already owned. But one day he bought a bigger house in a better land and he decided to move his entire collection across the open ocean.

He had already travelled ahead in an aircraft and was waiting in his new home for all his furniture and other possessions to arrive. And, although he was slightly nervous of flying, he had arranged for the wings to be sprinkled with salt and vinegar, thus making a *plain* crash impossible. He was rich enough for puns to have a beneficial effect in the real world, something that most people will never be able to afford. He waited in a rocking chair on a terrace.

This terrace was part of his front garden and it overlooked the beach and sea far below. One by one the ships bearing his possessions appeared on the horizon and docked at the jetty that extended out from the shore, servants and sailors scurried and scampered to unload the various cargoes and carry all the separate items up the steps carved in the side of the cliff and deposit them inside the house in the designated locations. While he rocked the hours away.

Within a few weeks most of his furniture and other possessions had been transferred from his old home to his new mansion. But his collection of genies was still on its way. It was such an extensive collection that it needed a ship all to itself, and this particular vessel was making slow progress because the captain had been ordered to take extra care to avoid bad weather. The ship had already delayed its departure thanks to adverse meteorological forecasts. Winter was coming!

The collection consisted of thousands of bottles and brass lamps and sealed jars in which a comprehensive variety of genies dwelled. There was at least one example of every possible kind of genie from all the cultures and mythologies in which they may be found. Most people may imagine they are only indigenous to deserts and oases, and the bazaars of Baghdad and Isfahan, but in fact they are universally distributed across the face of the world. They just happen to be very rare.

The collector, who was named Eugene, waited and waited for this final ship to arrive, but it never came. It had sunk in a storm and settled on the seabed far below and all the bottles had escaped back to the surface through a crack in the hull. They drifted in a great mass wherever the wind and waves and currents wanted them to go, and gradually they separated from each other and became isolated from their companions by vast expanses of ocean. An illusion of freedom.

The genies inside the bottles were generally genial and there was a good reason for this, namely that they now stood a better chance of winning true liberty for themselves than when they had formed Eugene's collection. In the collection they had been stuck with no hope of release but they finally had a chance of being washed up on some random shore, found by a person who was strolling the beach, and let loose. For the truth was that each genie had only one wish to dispose of before winning its freedom.

Genies generally grant three wishes. Eugene always used up two of them whenever he acquired a new addition, but never made a third wish, for he had no desire to let a genie escape him. He always wished for relatively modest things so that the world wouldn't be disrupted too much, and little by little he increased his wealth and power. If one wishes for a small business transaction to be successful then not too many things need to be influenced in order for this to actually happen.

But, if one wishes for the moon, the end result will be disaster. Too many of the forces that make life on Earth possible will have to change and all the careful balances of nature will be skewed. Not only will the wisher be crushed by the mass of the moon as it lands on him or her but all other living things will be seriously, and perhaps fatally, affected by the meeting of two enormous celestial bodies. Eugene was wise enough to be cautious. He was a slow and steady accumulator, a patient individual.

Therefore the total amount of wishes in his entire collection divided by two-thirds was the number of tiny steps it had taken to increase the success of his life over a period of many years. Then the genies were retired into the collection with a single unused wish that he never planned to exploit and this was a most frustrating situation for them. They resented him for it but could do nothing to help themselves, and so they lurked in their bottles, lamps and jars, and washed themselves morosely in the flow of time.

And now the collection was dispersed and there was hope again for them. Eugene, however, had hopes of his own that were in direct opposition to theirs. He decided to retrieve his collection genie by genie, and was willing to spend a lot of money in order to do so. He didn't really make much of a physical effort but he employed others to search for the genies on land and sea, for he suspected that some had already been washed up on the shore while the others were still adrift on the deeps.

So he spent most of his time on his rocking chair on the terrace in his garden and, while he waited for news about any genie that might be located, he indulged himself with luxurious food and drink. He nibbled chocolates and emptied his port decanter; then he emptied his starboard decanter too and moved onto gâteau. But he wasn't a fat man. He had once wished for a fast metabolism. The weeks passed and none of his hired men reported any success in the difficult search.

Then, one evening as he rocked the sunset to bed, the almost horizontal ray of the final flash of the top of the sinking sun struck something in the water and made it sparkle. Eugene was instantly on his feet. He hurried to the staircase hewn into the cliff and almost tumbled to his doom in his eagerness to reach the beach. The ink in my pen is about to run out so please excuse me while I search for a replacement... Yes, I still use a pen to write. I am absurdly old-fashioned.

This replacement pen is the last one in my possession and it would be dreadful if it also ran out of ink before I had told the entire tale so I really should abandon these unnecessary digressions. Eugene waded into the sea and snatched up the bottle that had found its way to him. It was indeed one of his genie bottles and he carried it carefully back to his house – the first specimen in a new collection – and positioned it proudly in the room originally designed for the display of his accumulated genies.

But it looked very forlorn there, on its own in a vast room, and over the next few days Eugene flirted with an idea that previously would have seemed unthinkable to him: namely, the uncorking of the solitary genie and the utilisation of the single remaining wish. Finally, he could resist the impulse no longer and he descended into that incongruously empty chamber, took hold of the bottle and released the genie, who poured out in the form of thick green smoke before congealing into his preferred anthropomorphic shape.

"I want my final wish," said Eugene.

The genie bowed deeply and resumed hovering. "Of course. Make it and set me free: this is my greatest desire. But..."

"But what?" frowned Eugene.

"Permit me to make the small observation that had you been a woman instead of a man, you might have been named Eugenie rather than Eugene, and in a story about genies that would have been even more apt. But the author of this text is clearly incapable of achieving the optimum aesthetic resonance in his work. Too bad. Now please kindly state what you want to wish for."

"I wish for all the other genies in my lost collection to find their way here so that the entire set might be regained."

"Minus myself, of course, so not *quite* entire."

Eugene shrugged. "I am bitter about this fact but what can I do? I am willing to sacrifice you in order to be reunited with the others. Your absence will then glare like a missing tooth in a mouth but, at the moment, I am facing a collection that is a single tooth in a wasteland of gum tissue. I must do what is best for me, even if it is not an ideal solution."

"Nonetheless, this wish is a very big wish."

"Indeed. The largest I have ever made."

"Therefore the consequences will be considerable and very difficult to calculate beforehand. It is only right to point this out."

Eugene sighed. "Grant my wish anyway."

The genie bowed again and waved his arms. "It is done," he announced with an enigmatic smile. "Farewell." And he drifted through the wall and vanished. Eugene exhaled, steadied his nerves, went back out onto the terrace and planted himself in his rocking chair, gazing out to sea. Against his better judgement he was hoping that the wish would work instantly and that a flotilla of bottles and jars would already be in the process of getting stranded on the sands below the dwelling.

But manipulation of the forces of the universe rarely produces immediate results and, in this case, the execution of the wish took time. The currents of all the oceans had to change, the winds too, and the disruption this caused to the climate and therefore civilisation was considerable. The global economy suffered greatly. But, very gradually, one by one, the bottles and lamps and jars returned to him and he took them to the special room and his collection grew to more than three-quarters of what it once had been.

These genies had been drifting hither and thither in all the seas of the world for a long time, remaining intact through storms and whirlpools, but suddenly they all found themselves being nudged by wavelets towards the same destination, which was the beach beneath Eugene's house. They arrived with a certain regularity and were snatched up – but then they stopped coming. He waited with an impatience even greater than before and he even cursed the genie who had granted this wish for a trickster.

"Why the delay?" he growled to himself, pacing the floor of the room where his collection was assembled. "The economy has crashed and I am almost ruined and to reclaim the missing genies is the only thing that can ever console me. I don't understand why they don't all return to me!"

A short time later they found him.

But Eugene had forgotten one crucial fact. Before he had made his wish, some of the genies had already found freedom. Some of the bottles, lamps and jars had smashed in collisions with ships or floating debris, or on rocks, or even against each other. The contents were released and *those* genies went home to the oases, lagoons and volcanoes they originally came from. Others were washed up on other shores and found by ordinary people walking on the beach who uncorked them out of curiosity and then...

Well, the genies had appeared and granted a single wish to those fortunate individuals, discharging their obligation to remain in our dimension. They had vanished into another realm, a parallel universe, a place where free genies enjoy themselves without the burden of having to grant wishes. These genies have retired from the stresses and tribulations of our cosmos. The last thing they want is to return to our reality, and in fact they never do, but Eugene had forced them to do exactly that.

So they came to him through the four walls of that room in which he stood, converging on him with great velocity and determination, and they were no longer very genial at all, he had almost no time to even begin to understand what was happening before it had already happened. They took an *ungenial* revenge. It might be supposed that they would imprison him in a bottle, lamp or jar, so that he might know how it feels; or even transform him into a sentient version of one of those objects...

But this solution seemed too simple to them, too unimaginative, and what they actually did was turn him into a writing implement: a pen with his soul as the ink inside it. One of those pens that have a tendency to get lost, to fall down the side of a sofa or roll under a chair and remain lost for years until they are suddenly needed as a replacement for one that has run out. I am glad that the one I am using still appears to have enough ink remaining for me to finish this story, in the most...

Najort Esroh

Before the full-sized wooden horse was built, Odysseus made a model to demonstrate the viability of the design to his comrades. Usually not much is said about this in the epics but it was a nicely done figure and long after the sack of Troy it somehow found its way into an antique shop in a faded seaside resort on the south coast of England. That's where I discovered it, on a shelf cluttered with cobwebbed bottles.

"How much for the toy horse?" I asked the darkness.

No reply. So I repeated the question.

But there was nothing lurking in the shadows other than more shadows and it seemed that the shop had no keeper. Maybe he had slipped out for a minute on an errand; or perhaps he had died behind the counter, deep in a neglected gloom so thick it could be spread on toast or used to creosote a fence. I picked up the horse and examined it more carefully. It was in a fair condition despite the passing of three millennia.

"I'm not for sale," it suddenly said.

As you may imagine, I was surprised by this outburst.

"You are alive?" I wondered.

"No, no, not at all. I'm an automaton."

And then it explained who it was and how it came to be in this place, a remarkable tale in itself, and I shared the joy and terror of its experiences. Of being carried back to Greece as a souvenir by a sailor, of ending up in the clutches of a Roman, then a Hun, then a Crusader, and so on passing from hand to hand down the centuries, crisscrossing the continent, finding a home in sundry bazaars, museums and taverns.

The horse paused to clear its throat.

"But I wasn't automated until 1571 and that was in Germany when my owner was a clockmaker of incredible skill. My voicebox is powered by a spring kept permanently wound tight thanks to the eternal fluctuations of barometric pressure. Before that time I was utterly mute and non-sentient, just a jumble of wooden slats and nails, nothing more. Jakob Kremkraker was the name of my liberator, my teacher."

"If this is true, then how do you remember all the things that happened to you before that year?" I demanded.

"Because the clockmaker included a memory into my mechanism that was already primed with my personal history. He was a very considerate man as well as an engineering genius."

"Will I find him mentioned in history books?"

"Unlikely. He kept his marvellous secrets to himself. He experimented with perpetual motion, and heavier-than-air flight but chiefly he preferred to enjoy a mild life among his timepieces. Herr Kremkraker has certainly remained obscure since then. I have no reason to lie to you; I'm merely a talking model horse, nothing more. I would visit his grave if I was sure he had one and if I knew where it might be."

"And if you could walk," I added.

"Oh, I can trot along if I must," the horse said. "But the effort depletes the tension in my spring faster than it can be wound up again, so I require frequent rests when I do move. Speech, on the other hand, is less wasteful of energy. I can talk to you all afternoon."

"On the other hand? On the other hoof, you mean!"

He failed to find my quip amusing.

"Would you *like* me to talk to you all afternoon?" he asked.

"I don't know. What do you intend to say?"

"That's up to you. Ask a question."

"Any question at all?"

He nodded and rolled his eyes. "Yes."

"Tell me, what is the strangest thing you've ever observed during your three thousand years of experience?"

He grinned at this and I saw that his tiny wooden teeth were varnished but rotten. They must have been chemically treated after starting to decay and not before. I therefore assumed that Herr Kremkraker had inherited a poor specimen, a battered ornament full of nothing but ancient air and he had reconstructed the model's exterior as well as inserting clockwork into the hollow belly, but the teeth were too far gone.

"It happened in the city of Troy..."

"Shortly after you were made?" I interrupted.

He swivelled his head to one side.

"Not that Troy but another. I'll try to explain more carefully. After the Greeks invaded and sacked the city the survivors fled in many directions. The most illustrious went west. One of them, Aeneas, founded Rome; and Brutus was responsible for Tours; Priam himself became the first ruler of the Franks; and the son of Memnon, who called himself Thor, established several of the Scandinavian kingdoms."

"But is any of that *real* history?" I quibbled.

The horse ignored my objection. "Some of these refugees gave to their new homes the name of the old, so from the destruction of one Troy came others. I visited a few and lived in one."

"Very well. Tell me about this new Troy."

"I ended up there after serving time as a paperweight on the desk of a captain's cabin; he was an explorer. When he retired, he cleared out all his possessions and relocated them into his new house. I was positioned on a windowsill overlooking the main square of the town. Although referred to as a city in official records, it was a fairly small settlement really. I had an excellent view of all the significant streets."

"Were the times troubled?"

"All times are that," he replied with a sigh.

"Wars? Plague? Famine?"

"Not quite. Not that time. It was mutiny."

"The poor of the town rebelling against the rich? Agitation because of unfair taxation? Was that the case?"

"No, the horses, that's who!"

"A mutiny among the horses of New Troy?"

"Yes, yes, and why not?"

I nodded sombrely. Horses are often used as slaves, treated very badly by their owners, underfed and abused, worked to death, and this has been true for thousands of years, ever since they were domesticated by the first man who had the idea of leaping onto the back of one and shouting, "Gee up!" or the equivalent of that in the language he spoke. It is not so surprising that horses should revolt.

The teller of the tale fell silent.

"Did they break down the doors of their cramped stables and run amok in the narrow streets?" I prompted him.

The toy horse blinked rapidly, as if awakening from a thick and sticky dream, and replied, "No, they were cleverer than that. They had recently heard a story about men who constructed a wooden horse in order to get into a city and they saw no reason why they shouldn't try something very similar but opposite in order to get out of theirs. This story is overfamiliar to your kind but quite new to the equine race."

"I understand perfectly," I said.

"They built an artificial man, a wooden giant."

"And they hid inside it?"

"You mustn't attempt to anticipate me."

"I humbly apologise," I said.

"The horses called the giant man Najort Esroh."

"What does that mean?" I asked.

"Merely a name. What do names mean? They mean only themselves. Any other meaning isn't important."

"I take your point. Please continue your narration."

"Yes, I will. From my vantage I could see what transpired. One misty morning, the citizens were astounded to confront the giant man standing in the main square. They guessed quickly what was happening and they pushed and dragged the thing far outside the city walls. They knew that mutinous horses were concealed within and it took every denizen of the settlement to shift the vast figure outside."

"Including the women and children?" I pressed.

"Of course. Every inhabitant."

"And what happened when Najort Esroh was expelled?"

"They set it on fire. Burned it!"

"And killed all the horses inside?" I gasped.

The toy horse laughed, a rasping sound. "No, for there were no horses within. They had played a double bluff, remaining behind in their stables and waiting for the city to be evacuated."

"Ah, so the horses were now in control of Troy?"

"Indeed. They locked the gates and left the foolish citizens outside in a light rain that came to hiss against the charred embers of the giant. When the men and women wanted to return, the horses refused to let them back in. I witnessed everything and it was the strangest thing in my three thousand year history. You asked and I answered."

I digested his odd account for a few minutes.

"But how did the horses get to learn of Odysseus' trick?"

The toy horse snickered. "Me!"

"So you helped your own kind, even though you are artificial and they were real; and this happened after Herr Kremkraker automated you? And that's how you were able to urge the real horses to rebellion, by speaking to them with your mechanical voice."

"No, no, it happened before I ever met him!"

"But you said you were dumb then, non-sentient, a simple toy with no more intelligence than any dead object!"

"And so I was. Why are you so shocked by this?"

"It makes the tale *more* impossible."

"Jakob Kremkraker gave me a personal history but I don't know how he researched it. Perhaps he simply made it up. All I know is that I recall the incident very clearly. I also have some concrete evidence. Before they built the full-sized giant man, the horses made a model to demonstrate the viability of the design. Look behind me."

I could see almost nothing in the gloom but I reached out and groped with my clumsy fingers. Sure enough, there was another toy there, further back on that shelf, a wooden man, a miniature giant. "How much for this toy?" I asked the horse without irony.

"I'm not for sale," the giant suddenly said.

I left that shop in a hurry, not because I was frightened by the peculiar nature of the items inside, but because I was late for an appointment with my mechanic. I am the Lord Mayor of this faded seaside resort and I need regular winding. Because I can't reach to insert the brass key into the hole in the middle of my back on my own, a reliable mechanic with big hands is essential for my continued wellbeing.

Travels with my Antinomy

There is no absolute truth. Or is there? I went travelling with my knapsack and curiosity over a range of mountains far from home. I was looking for a village I had once been told about, a village where I might find something I had lost that was neither my senses nor my virginity. It was a long way but ways are longer often than this one so complain I did not.

At last, when the sun was setting beautifully in the west – where always it sets, at least to my knowledge – I saw the village spread below me. It was tinted rose and purple at that hour and I hurried down the slope towards it. There was a solitary tavern with an oaken door that yielded to my knocking. I asked for a room for the night and was given the attic.

After resting for a short time, I went down to where there was a blaze and mugs of cider available for me to slake my thirst. And, while engaged in the arts of stretching my legs afore the flames and sharpening my innards on the brew, I asked the barman, who seemed an agreeable fellow, if there were any other men hereabouts who had a beard just like mine.

"Not only not like yours, but not like anyone else's."

"There are no beards here?"

"Every man in this village, Señor, is clean shaven."

"You have a very busy barber."

"Ah, the barber shaves only the men who do not shave themselves. That is the law among us who dwell here."

"And no man ever neglects to shave or be shaved?"

"That is correct, Señor."

Then I knew I was in the village I was seeking, the village where all men are smooth cheeked and either shave themselves or are shaved by the barber. So I tugged at my beard, the beard of a wanderer, sipped my cider and felt the warmth radiate outward from my body toward the fire; as if two different kinds of heat were about to meet and mingle.

"In that case," I said lightly, "who shaves the barber?"

"Shaves the barber, Señor!"

"Yes indeed. Who?"

The barman sighed and tapped his nose but it was mercifully clear he did not yet regard me as a troublemaker, merely as a stranger, an ordinary man who had finally asked the awkward but inevitable question he had been expecting for years, if not decades. He poured a mug of cider for himself and he shrugged and then came over to sit next to me.

"The barber has two choices, Señor. He can shave himself or he can go to the barber to be shaved. There is only one barber in the village, so if he decides to visit the barber he will visit himself. In other words, he really has one choice and it is not even a choice. He must shave himself. But, by tradition he shaves only the men who do not shave themselves."

"So he cannot shave himself?"

"As you say, Señor. But he cannot grow a beard because there are only clean shaven men dwelling in this village."

"That is the paradox," I replied. "I had it once upon a time but I lost it in my youth. Now I have found it again."

"What will you do with it, now you have it?"

"Take it with me when I leave."

"But we need it, Señor; it is the only one we have. This is the village with only one barber, who is male, and who shaves all those, and only those, who do not shave themselves. If you take the paradox with you, what will we have left? And he is a very heavy man, too heavy for you to lift. I also believe he will fight back and perhaps slash open your throat."

"My presence here spoils the paradox anyway."

He gazed at my beard a long time.

"Yes, Señor, I suppose it does. But if you are gone in the morning, it will be repaired. The paradox will thus only be suspended for one night. And, in fact, you cannot take the paradox away with you, because while you are here there is no paradox. The paradox only works if every man in the village is clean shaven and you most definitely are not that."

This was true. I realised that I had been questing for a rainbow or horizon, something that would move further away and out of reach the nearer I got to it. I understood that this was a logical consequence of my situation and that only one of two courses of action would help. I would either have to shave myself or else go to the barber to be shaved. So I said:

"May I borrow a razor from you tonight?"

"You may not, Señor."

"Then I will have to visit the barber tomorrow morning."

The barman lowered his head.

I finished my cider and went up to my room. There was a desk in a corner of the attic and a chair. I did not feel sleepy and so I decided to update my travel journal. I opened my knapsack and took it out, together with my quill and bottle of ink, which I arranged neatly on the desk. I heard footsteps outside and I went to the little window and peered cautiously out.

The barman was hurrying down the street in the moonlight. I guessed that he was going to rouse the barber and tell him to hide when I called round to see him in the morning. I would not easily get a shave here, but, if I did manage to, I would certainly not be permitted to take the barber back with me. I would have to remain here, a prisoner, imbibing cider.

Shaking my head ruefully, because that is my favourite way of shaking it among the several methods I am aware of, I sat down and opened my journal to a new page. Then I dipped my quill into the ink and began writing. I told of my trek over the mountains and how I... but no, those were not the words that now lay on the page before me. I blinked at them.

My blinking was so rapid and my eyelashes are so long that the ink dried more quickly than it would have done had another man penned those words. It appeared that I had written an account of how to tend horses in a stable. Had the rigours and stresses of my journey muddled my brains? I began again on a clean page but once again the words tricked me.

Now I had written about gathering windfall apples in the orchards on the edge of the village. I tried a third time. Now my account told of milking goats on the slopes where the wild flowers grew.

A fourth and fifth time, a sixth time, seventh, eighth...

It was peculiar and unnerving.

At last, in agitation, I got up and paced the room, creaking warped boards with muddy boots. I paused only at the window and looked out again. The moon was still shining brightly and I could see the whole village. In every house just one window was illuminated and it always belonged to the highest room of that house. They were lit by lamps like mine.

And men were behind each one of those windows; and some of these men were sitting at desks of their own, writing in journals identical to mine, but most of them simply stood there, faces pressed to the glass, and gazed in my direction and grinned when they saw me looking back. And then I realised that I was part of another paradox, one related to the first.

There is a village with just one professional scribe, who is bearded, and in this village every man keeps a careful account of the day's events, and does this by doing one of two things. Either he writes his own journal or the scribe writes it on his behalf. The scribe writes only the journals of the men who do not write their own. Who writes the scribe's journal?

I knew that if I took my journal with me when I left, as I was planning to do, I would free the paradox from this prison. It would be my companion on all my future travels, like a woman but easier to read, to flick through, to replace or forget; not at all like a woman really. I blew out the lamp and went to bed and I dreamed only once of a looming shiny blade.

The Bubble Bursts

To live and work in a giant bubble, far beneath the surface of the ocean, seemed like a good idea to Ruth and me. There would be all sorts of opportunities down there that we didn't have up here, and many chances to further both our careers. Exactly what forms those opportunities and chances might take we couldn't actually specify but that didn't matter.

The important thing was that we had made a positive decision. We were going to leave the city that had been our prison for so many years and relocate to a contrived subaquatic paradise at a depth of some two kilometres. It wasn't just a case of deciding to go because there were bureaucratic hoops to jump through, and a lot of application forms to fill out.

Interviews too. But we were successful in the end, surely because we were still young and vibrant. Neither of us could swim but that didn't matter. It was explained to us that the interior of the bubble was utterly dry and that, even if we could swim, it wouldn't make any difference in a disaster. It was just too deep to expect survivors if anything went wrong.

That reassured us and we submitted to the operation that was necessary to help us integrate. I know what you are thinking. No, it wasn't fins or gills they grafted onto us but wings. They replaced our human bones with hollow ones made from some new material with a name I never learned to pronounce, and our feathers were silky smooth but rip-proof.

Ruth looked extremely attractive when she flapped her wings and took to the air. I soared after her and we played an erotic game of chase for a quarter of an hour before the chief surgeon clucked his tongue and said, "That's not really the most appropriate sort of behaviour in a hospital, is it?" Then we were discharged and told to await transportation to the bubble.

A few days later it came: a submarine on wheels that picked us up from our old home, with its sagging roof and mouldy walls, and rumbled with us down the broken streets of the decaying metropolis to the dark river where it slid beneath the oily waters with a grateful plop, watched by listless pedestrians on bridges, and then continued onwards to the estuary.

Beyond the estuary lay the open sea, and a week or so later we had reached the middle point of the ocean where the bubble was located. Down and downer went the submarine, the captain making sonar noises as it did so because the real sonar was broken, until we felt a gentle judder and knew we had hit something more solid than water but just as yielding.

"We are passing through the air locks," the captain said.

There were no portholes so we had to take his word for it, and we did, but we gave it back later, when it was too late. Ruth flapped her wings in excitement and I did the same and our shiny feathers reflected the lights of a dozen consoles and devices scattered about the bridge of the submarine. "Don't do that, you are making a cold breeze," the captain growled.

Eventually the submarine came to a halt and the hatch was opened in the conning-tower and we were permitted to disembark. We found ourselves on a platform in the exact centre of the bubble and this platform was held aloft by a pair of rotors that span in nacelles below us. But how had the submarine reached this platform from the side of the bubble?

It took only a single blink to discern the truth of the matter. It dangled by a hook from a cord and the cord was strung from the platform to the airlock far to the side. It had slid down the length of this cord like a cucumber on a zip wire, if you will pardon such a useless comparison. It would return on another cord to a slightly lower air-lock. An ingenious system!

But we were given no time to ponder this or anything else, for a man now fluttered down to us and shook our hands. He was the janitor, he explained, and was responsible for more things than such a humble title might lead us to suspect. For instance, he was also the political officer here and was charged with ensuring that no one living in the bubble caused trouble.

"But I don't think I'll have any difficulties with you," he said, looking us carefully up and down and nodding happily.

"What is our work?" we asked.

"Anything at all. Just play and enjoy yourselves," he said

affably. "For that is work as useful as any other; but, if you wish to grow food or clean surfaces or teach children, please do so. It is voluntary."

"Will you show us to our new home?"

He wagged a finger. "Ah! That is the mistake that all newcomers make. No citizen of the bubble has a home of their own. Everything here is shared equally among everyone. You may go anywhere, partake of anything, sleep and eat and bathe where you like, provided the facilities for doing such functions are present and available. The bubble is a commune."

"That's a breath of fresh air!" exclaimed Ruth.

But the janitor glowered at her and said in a sharp whisper, "Do mind your language and think before you speak; or even better, don't think at all. There are some topics that are taboo down here. They may have been perfectly acceptable up on *terra firma* but simply won't do now. Fresh air being one of them. That's a mighty sore subject for many inhabitants."

After delivering this rebuke he became friendly again and bowed deeply, a man with no greater desire than to look after the citizens in his care. He flapped away and we watched him depart with admiration at his flying technique, for he had mastered the art of using minimal energy and glided for rather long periods between each beat of his shimmering wings.

It was time to explore the bubble and examine our new home, familiarising ourselves with as much of it as we could and getting to know our neighbours, so we leapt off the platform into space. All the structures in the bubble had rotors and suspended themselves in mid air without touching the sides. Some platforms were circular, others were square, triangular, polygonal or irregular. A few were bowl shaped or resembled saddles or pyramids.

Many of the platforms contained gardens or were entirely one big garden or orchard; others were crammed with buildings, including apartments, shops and schools. There were unsavoury platforms too, full of narrow alleyways, lurking shadows, and an essence of menace. Something for everyone. We were very civil to the folks we met and they were equally polite.

"Are you enjoying life in the bubble?" we asked them.

Always they shrugged. "We don't know yet, for we haven't been here long enough to reach a final decision, but our instinct tells us that soon we will be able to give a positive response to your question."

"When did you arrive?" we wondered.

"Just now. On the submarine. What about you?"

This baffled us. And yet it was the reply we always received. "But we were the only passengers on the vessel. We stood on the bridge with the captain and all the other crew members. Where were you?"

"We were on the bridge with the captain!" they insisted.

After much thought, Ruth and I came to the conclusion that the submarine had contained *many* bridges and *many* captains all sealed off from each other and that it had been designed in this manner to give every passenger the feeling he or she was special. Was this a sinister truth or did it simply mean that the authorities were more considerate of human feelings?

"It seems," said Ruth, "that no one was here before our arrival. We are the first to arrive and yet the illusion was created that we were joining an established society. I wonder when the janitor came?"

I advised her against asking him directly. He seemed stern despite the smile he generally wore on his leathery face. When Ruth and I flew close to the sides of the bubble he appeared from nowhere to block our way. "That is not permitted. It would be a grotesque shame if you were to smudge the stunning view by pressing your hands against the glass," he explained.

In truth there was almost no light outside, and we saw only the reflection of the interior of the bubble, but I said in astonishment, "The walls are made only of glass? But the pressure on them must be huge!"

"Diamond," corrected the janitor, and then he laughed.

"But you said glass," pointed out Ruth.

"It is easier," he spat, and he glowered at us until we retreated. Very rarely in the aftermath of this incident did we dare approach the sides of the bubble. In conversation with our neighbours we learned that nobody had managed to touch it. One ventured the unorthodox opinion that there was no solid wall at all, that our bubble was just made of ordinary air.

"It could be a natural bubble," he declared.

I pondered this but could think of nothing clever to say. Then Ruth had an idea that she put forward partly in jest. "If we all breathe in at the same time, the bubble should contract slightly and this movement ought to be noticed. That will settle the issue once and for all. Inhale!"

And we did but it made no difference. The bubble remained exactly as big as before. But I couldn't shake off the notion we were living in an air bubble and that our government had tricked us into relocating to a place with no future and no inherent strength. One evening, while swinging on a hammock on a platform designed to resemble a beach, I woke in a panic and shook Ruth, who lay across me like a pair of trousers filled with shells.

"If this is a natural air bubble we should be rising and we aren't doing that, which disproves the hypothesis," I gasped. "Unless time has been slowed to such an extreme degree that it only appears to be static. But not even our government could slow a rising air bubble this size."

"No," agreed Ruth, "but it might be capable of altering our time perception so that we only believe it's not rising."

"Do you think that during the operation...?"

Ruth nodded. "Yes, they messed with our brains as well as our bones. With a few scalpel cuts here and there they accelerated our time sense so that a fraction of a second now seems like a year. We *are* in a natural air bubble after all, vented from some ancient cavern or tunnel beneath the seabed, and we are rising without guessing the fact. They have deceived us."

"What a sneaky way of reducing the population!" I snorted. "But they will be in trouble when the bubble breaks the surface of the ocean, as it must do. That is when the truth will come out. We will fly to the nearest landmass and let it be known we are the victims of a cruel trick."

"They won't ever allow that to happen," sighed Ruth.

"What do you mean?" I croaked.

"They will burst the bubble long before then and drown us."

"How will they burst it?" I cried.

"They already have," said Ruth, and she gestured in the direction of the air locks on the side of the bubble. I frowned.

"They will open the locks and let the water pour in?"

"No, no!" she breathed, and then she added, "There are no air locks at all, merely puncture wounds. Don't you realise that the submarine was the needle to burst the bubble? So it has already been popped. In fact it was popped by the act of delivering us into the interior. We just haven't realised it yet and we might not actually experience it for many generations."

"It depends on how much our time sense was accelerated."

"Yes, I'm rather afraid it does."

"And there's no way of knowing that?"

"I don't think so. It would require very careful and precise observation and calculation; and I doubt the janitor will permit anything along those lines. So the best thing is simply to continue our lives as best we can, knowing that they might come to an abrupt end at any instant."

"In other words, exactly like life up above?"

"Yes, indeed," she answered, and I had the impression that her words were encapsulated in a large speech bubble.

And so we continued to act as if nothing was wrong, and maybe, in a sense, nothing *was* wrong. Nothing, at any rate, that hadn't already been wrong in our former lives in that depressing sordid city. We all live in bubbles of some kind or another, irrespective of the shape or consistency of our surroundings. Even those men who occupy the interior of the submarine that popped our little cosmos, the plurality of captains and crew, are *enbubbled*.

There is no such word and I'm acutely aware of this.

Have I failed to be convincing?

It doesn't matter. If there is a point to this tale it will burst the meaning and spray the words all over you, reader.

A Dame Abroad

She was a dame. She talked like a dame, moved like a dame, smelled like a dame, breathed like a dame, slept like a dame, yawned like a dame, coughed like a dame, dusted like a dame, cooked like a dame, had the metabolism of a dame, knew about as much astrophysics as a dame would, had a selection of hats typical of a dame. She was a dame.

No doubt about it. A dame through and through. Her hips were as wide and curvy as a concert piano and her feet were like pedals, so if you stood on one while she was talking her voice would become a swelling overlapping echo and if you stood on the other her voice would be muted and soft. But no man could play her well. She was out of tune.

Her lipstick was a dame's lipstick and it was the colour of the edges of a bullet wound or some sort of massive head trauma. It could even be said that it was the shade of blood that gushes from a busted lip. It wasn't the lipstick of a homunculus or panda. She left her apartment and swayed down the length of this sentence to the end of the paragraph.

Her hips kept getting stuck between the margins of the story – that's how wide they were – but she finally arrived on the street and headed downtown, a part of town under uptown. She was going there because the plot told her to and she had no choice. She was without choice, without even a dame's choice, but she had everything else a dame should.

Yes, she was a dame. She was also a broad. A broad is a certain kind of dame and, in fact, I don't think there's any difference between them but I'm not really an expert. Maybe there is a miniscule arcane difference, something to do with the atoms of the ankles. Who knows? I don't. Maybe you do. Maybe you are a dame or broad who knows. Well done.

I am a private eye. That's who I am. I used to be a public eye but people got upset and complained to the authorities about my appearance. They didn't like to see a gigantic eye rolling along the pavement towards them. It disturbed them that the rest of my head was missing, that I had no body or limbs, that I was just an eye with the diameter of a cottage.

So the authorities forced me to go private and encased me inside a brick pyramid and now I blink out near the summit of the structure and you can find me on the hill overlooking the town. I don't solve many cases these days, to be honest, but that's because I'm too busy living a fantasy life. In my fantasy life I'm a man with all my parts fully functional.

These daydreams are starting to occupy all my waking hours. I imagine that my name is Sergio Surges and I have a moustache so big that a policeman can conceal himself inside it. This is helpful when confronting lethal criminals with their deeds. For example, at this precise instant I'm about to enter a bar where a notorious gangster is playing pool.

I watch him splashing about with the rubber ducks and toy boats but it's rude and dangerous to stare so I turn away and order a drink from the barman, who happens to be a midget pygmy. "Rum."

Pygmies are quite small already but the midgets among them are really tiny, no higher than the knees of a freak spider.

"What kind?" he asks.

"The kind that begins with the letter B," I reply.

"Brandy, you mean?"

"Sure! Make it a double on the rocks."

He places a selection of pebbles on the bar and slowly pours the alcohol over them. I nod and pay him. I also tip him. Over the edge of the tall stool on which he stands. He plummets through an open trapdoor that leads to a very long passage that passes through the world all the way back to where he came from, which is the Pygmalion Republic.

That passage is so long it goes on for umpteen hundred thousand pages. This is the highly condensed version.

"What did you do that for?" cries the notorious gangster.

"He was corrupt," I answer coolly.

"And what the hell do you think *you* are?"

"I am Sergio Surges, the private eye who is more than just an eye, and I am not corrupt at all, partly because this is just a daydream, but I know for an unchecked fact that he, the barman, was taking bribes from you in order to let wicked things happen on the premises."

"Oh yeah? What sort of wicked things, buddy?"

"No idea. I don't bother with little details like that. It's too much effort. Maybe he allowed you to fight the shadows of gibbons on that wall over there. Or maybe he let you to use a freshly baked pizza as an indoor Frisbee and the toppings were pineapple and chocolate."

"Is this some kind of joke?"

"Do I look like an Englishman, a Scotsman and an Irishman? Of course it's no joke. You are under arrest."

"I'm going to kill ya with my heater!"

He gets out of the pool and plugs a portable electric heater into a socket on the wall, taking care not to drip on the wires, and waits for the filaments to start glowing. But he is far too slow. The policeman in my moustache instantly reveals himself and blasts him with a truncheon that is actually a mini-bazooka and I watch him burst like applause.

A round of. Very satisfying.

The door swings open and the dame walks in like a baby grand. My jaw drops open. What is she doing here?

"This is my daydream. Get out!" I bellow.

Her lipsticked lips curl in a sneer that is half smile. "A daydream? Fine. I am a day-dame so I belong here."

I despise it when confusions arise and unplanned things happen in what is supposed to be my personal fantasy. I usually escape them by going into the next level of daydream, by closing my eyes and imagining I am Hugo Lobes, a private eye with ears so large that a couple of pygmy midgets can hide behind each one, both armed with blowpipes.

I am sitting on the top deck of a tram and reading the newspaper and the front page headline screams at me that a terrible gangster is sitting downstairs on the same tram at this very moment, so I get up to make my way down the curving set of metal steps but my way is blocked by a woman who is coming up. To my dismay I recognise her...

The dame! She followed me into this fantasy!

"This is most unfair!" I roar.

"I go wherever I please," she retorts.

"But I thought you didn't have a choice. It said earlier in this story that you were a dame without choice."

"Precisely. I have *no choice* but to go where I please."

"You mean that your free will is—"

"Predetermined," she says.

So I vanish into the third level of daydream, the level where I am Bogie Clubs, a private eye with such a big mouth that gibbons could bake pizzas in there without anyone getting suspicious, and I am on the deck of a cruise ship that is heading to the Bermuda Shorts, a pair of islands where a gangster has taken refuge in one of the deep pockets.

A steward approaches. "Would monsieur care for a drink?"

"Gin," I answer languidly.

"What kind?" he asks in a high voice.

"The kind that begins with the letter V," I reply.

"Vodka, you mean?"

"No thanks. Vermouth please."

But he doesn't go to fetch me my beverage. Instead he pulls off his cap and unbuttons his jacket to reveal—

The dame! It's the dame again! That damned dame!

I vanish into the next level.

Now I am Griswald Jerkins, the private eye with a chin dimple so deep that a tram driver with a halberd could conceal himself and pop out and swing it most effectively at the drop of a hat, especially one of those very heavy hats that make a clanging noise when it lands. I am furiously pedalling a unicycle up a mountain path in pursuit of a gangster.

Another unicycle catches up with me, draws level.

The rider is the dame again!

I escape into the next level. I am Morton Punchbowl and—

The dame, the dame, the dame!

Through all the daydreams she follows me and each subsequent fantasy has slightly less detail in it, is less fleshed out, sparser, bleaker, less real then the one that preceded it, and each private eye is less convincing because I've spent less time working on their identities and environments than I might have done. But fleeing this way is my only hope.

Here's a short list of some of the private eyes I become:

Mickey Stains.

Hercule Pompbustus.

Heston Furball.

Flippy Masters.

Duckbreath Chumptaster.

Ratleg Smashy.
Occidental Brushtooth.
Ajax van Scruba.
Chickpea Bunkerlove.
Zippy Buttons.
Gusty Nuts.
Lemontoe Thumbrag.
And then I run out of daydreams and run out of names and run out of big body parts and run out of time, energy and space, and I find myself, as I'm sure you have already anticipated, completing the circle, closing the loop and becoming myself again: a colossal eyeball inside a pyramid, and I glance down and see her climbing the hill towards me.

"Leave me alone!" I scream.

"I will now," she says. "I just wanted to go on a journey, that's all, out of this story and around the world. I wanted to go abroad. I was a dame but a stay-at-home dame. And now I've been abroad, so I'm a dame abroad and a broad at home, and it feels just fine. I climbed up here to thank you but also to ask your advice. I really need to know."

"What is it?" I am frantic to get rid of her. I'll say anything to make her go away, answer any question. And then it comes, she hits me with it, and I'm more acutely aware than ever before that she's a dame, that she has the soul of a dame, the heart of a dame, the plot of a dame, the metaphors of a dame, the grammar of a dame, the power of a dame.

"How *do* you curl your lashes?"

A Real Nowhere Man

I was bored with my home, my friends and my job, so I took a few days off to go walking by myself. It was a relief to be away from the telephone and to give my voice a rest. But I had not hiked far when I spied a figure approaching from the opposite direction, a lean man in a tattered cloak who wore enormous blue spectacles on his nose. I hoped we would pass without exchanging a word, and I even turned my face away from him, but he hailed me the moment he saw me, with these words:

"Tell me, O stranger, about the lands you have come from, the regions you have lately trodden with your feet, for you travel north and I journey south, and so you already know everything that lies in wait for me. Relate everything you can, omit no detail, about the customs of the people, the buildings and bazaars, the foodstuffs and textiles, the beliefs and biases, the climate and geography, the artworks and music, the laws and festivals."

"I beg your pardon?" I cried, for he was still distant.

At much closer range he repeated his request and I shook my head. "You are the first to refuse me!" he spluttered in wonder.

"Frankly," said I, "my mood for talking is in abeyance. I sell insurance over the telephone for a living. I care not to speak in my spare time, if I can avoid it, and the main reason I am out here is to enjoy the silence and isolation."

"I am sorry," he muttered dismally.

He looked so crestfallen with the shreds of his cloak hanging around him that I relented, at least in part, and said, "But I am prepared to listen to your story, if you have one, and I will do so with good grace. Is that enough?"

"Will you provide comments at regular intervals?" he pressed.

I replied in the negative and watched as he adjusted his spectacles and considered my terms with a frown that threatened to split his weathered forehead down the middle. Then he arrived at a decision, nodded once and commenced his tale:

"Many years ago, I was gripped with a powerful desire to travel the world. I wanted to see all of it, every inch, and this urge was so intense and so impossible to achieve that I fell suddenly ill. A fever burned my limbs for days and I lay gasping on a mattress on my balcony, unable to conduct any of my normal business affairs. The people who passed in the street called up advice and the irony was that they suggested travel to distant lands as a cure, unaware that dreams of far places had caused my sickness in the first place.

"When my fever subsided and I could move freely again I was astonished to discover that my friends had raised a sum of money between them to make a long voyage feasible for me. Touched by this generosity, but curiously disheartened at the same time, for reasons I will explain in a moment, I wasted many days debating what to do next. I finally decided to conceal the bag of gold coins in a secret place, at the bottom of the opaque waters of the foulest fountain in my city, and I set off almost penniless just before dawn on the longest day of the year.

"The streets were deserted as I left my house and the outlines of the buildings were firmer and more definite in the early light than they seemed at a later hour, an illusion that confirmed the feeling inside me that I had finally awoken into reality after a lifetime of sleeping on my feet. Even the shadows had a clarity and precision that delighted me and my pace was rapid in response to my general glee. Out of my city I went, into the hills, and did not rest until noon when I stopped under the shelter of a boulder to unwrap and devour my lunch.

"Now I will confess something that might make me seem unduly naïve or perverse, namely that I wanted to proceed in this simple style, like a carefree gypsy, for the entire duration of my journey. It was a romantic notion I had of myself, a foolish one too, but I believed I had the stamina to truly become what I wanted to be. To travel and lodge in comfort seemed a betrayal of my aspirations, and that is why I rejected the funds given by my friends, though I had no wish to hurt their feelings. They would never know of my poverty until I returned, eventually, to reclaim my treasure and pass my old age in luxury, saturated with worldly experiences.

"Naturally, this was a gross misjudgement on my part. Walking everywhere in one pair of shoes and sleeping rough in all seasons is horribly taxing; a way of life that toughens the body and mind in one way but weakens both in others. I became a beggar, a scavenger, a thief, but by the time I was at my lowest ebb I was already too far from my home city to contemplate an easy return. Plus I could not bear the thought of losing face in front of my friends and neighbours. I resolved to keep travelling but with an adjustment to my procedure, an adjustment that would reduce the area to be covered by a fellow now in a state of malnutrition, but without loss of knowledge of far places..."

Although I had planned to remain silent during his tale, I found myself asking, "And how did you accomplish this?"

He winked behind his pale blue lenses, first his right eye, then his left. "I used proxies! My system is simplicity itself and has served me admirably ever since, or at least until I met you. I no longer hope to visit in person every land in the world. Instead I walk in a straight line – as straight as possible – until I meet a stranger coming the other way. I hail him and ask for information regarding the lands that are ahead of me but behind him. When I have heard everything there is to be said, I commit all the details to memory and then I abruptly change my direction.

"I change my direction always by ninety degrees, no more or less, so my progress consists of a series of right angles. The question you are about to ask is: how do I decide to turn left or right? First, I ask the stranger for a low value coin, then I toss this and consult the result. Heads means right, tails means left. If the stranger refuses to give me any charity, I use another method: the direction of the wind, the croaking of frogs, there are innumerable ways of choosing. I never turn back, never retrace my steps – that is a rule I refuse to break. The ground I tread must always be new.

"You consider me a little cracked in the head? But my system is an effective method of travelling mostly by hearsay. For a poor man it is a beautiful abridgment and compression of the great outside. It saves my poor bones much toil and my feet much wear. I see what I can see with my own eyes but I also borrow, in a manner of speaking, the eyes of those who have gone to places I never have and never will. This is not cheating, it is merely a form of good management. And one day, purely by chance, I will find that I have gone in a giant loop. I will see my home city on the horizon and enter it with a light heart, my long journey completed, my ambition fulfilled.

"And that is why I asked you to tell me about the places you have just come from, so that I might change my direction again at this very spot, heading east or west depending on the toss of the coin for which I would ask. But as you are disinclined to talk to me, I will pass you and continue south until I meet another traveller who is more obliging. Nonetheless I wish to thank you for your patience and attention. Who knows how long I must continue in this manner? I am exploring a maze with no real walls, the corners I turn are invisible, and the centre of this labyrinth is also the place where I entered. So now I will bid you farewell and leave you in peace."

He took a step forward and I held up my hands. "Wait!" I cried.

"Yes?" he wondered.

"Your story has touched me," I declared, "and I will save you the trouble of tramping any further in that direction. Behind me lies a high range of mountains and beyond the mountains is a vast plain and at the centre of the plain stands an extinct volcano. In the crater of this volcano is a lake and at the centre of the lake is an island on which has been built a shining pyramid. The pyramid in hollow and full of stairways that lead to terraces where musicians play strange instruments through the night. They do this in a vain attempt to stir the volcano into life, to awaken it, to cause it to explode and propel the pyramid into the sky and towards the stars. For such is their faith."

"That is very curious," he replied, "and I am pleased to learn of it. Now I will beg a coin from you in order to change my direction."

I reached into my pocket and found my smallest coin. He accepted it and threw the flimsy disc high, catching it in his palm and squinting. "Tails. That means I go east." And he turned and made ready to set off.

"Wait again!" I called to his profile.

"What?" he muttered.

"There is no point travelling east," I explained, "for I have also been there and can tell you what it is like. The ground becomes damper and damper until you enter a stinking marsh. There are no cities to be found, but men build nests from reeds and the women lay eggs just like wading birds. Childbirth is an incomprehensible notion to those people. Also they speak the language of snakes and all words, even those of welcome, are a hiss."

"Utterly bizarre!" was his response, "but I thank you again for this information. According to my principles I will travel west instead."

"But I have also been there," I quickly added, "and I can inform you that it consists of a steadily rising slope that becomes steeper and steeper by imperceptible degrees until it is a vertical wall. So gradually does the gradient increase that the unfortunate wanderer does not realise he is walking up a sheer face until he stops for a rest. At that moment gravity takes over and he plunges back down to a messy doom."

At this the man with the blue spectacles made no audible comment but I thought he mouthed the words, "I am stuck." Certainly his expression seemed to confirm this interpretation, but I am no expert at the reading of lips and could not be absolutely certain. He glanced left, right, forwards and back, shuffled a few paces one way, then another, but always returned to the same lonely spot. I smiled and raised my hand in a salute.

Then I briskly turned on my heel and hurried back the way I had come. But after half an hour I had second thoughts and looked over my shoulder. He was still there, a forlorn dot. I sighed and returned to him and I will always remember the look on his face, the indecision and bewilderment. Then he suddenly blurted:

"I cannot move... My rules! I am stuck!"

I nodded, pleased my earlier guess had been proved correct. "May I have my coin back?" I asked. He handed it over mutely.

I turned again and doubled my pace, my heart thumping,

until I reached the city that was my home. With luck I would never need to return to my boring job and boring friends. Three outrageous but simple lies had freed me from the prison of my former life. Only one crucial task remained. I made straight for the foulest fountain, glanced around to confirm nobody was watching, and dipped my arm into the slimy waters as far as my elbow. The bag of gold was there and now it was mine.

Gold, Myrrh and Frankenstein

"What's the name of the play?"

"It's called 'Horseplay' and is about horses at play. At least that's what it should be about with a title like that."

"I looked in the newspaper for a review but couldn't find one anywhere. I don't think it *has* been reviewed yet."

"I don't trust reviewers myself. They are a snooty bunch with agendas of their own. Let's go and watch it anyway and make up our own minds. It's better than staying indoors again, isn't it?"

"I suppose so. Come on, then. To the theatre!"

The streets were deserted.

Myrrh and Gold walked from one puddle of light to the next and dried their photon-drenched feet in the shadows where no lamps on poles glowed. It wasn't cold but there was a little persistent wind that blew dust around corners, like granulated businessmen late for work.

"No one goes to the theatre these days."

"I don't think anybody does anything at all anymore."

"Apart from us maybe?"

"Not even us," grumbled Gold.

The houses that they passed had no windows. Or rather they had none facing onto the street. Fashions had changed. All windows now faced inwards onto central courtyards that were completely surrounded by the four sides of a building. It was the way it was done now.

They reached the centre of the town in about twenty minutes. There were no shops and no pedestrians, no traffic and no policemen, no signs of human life and none of any other kind. It was a perfectly intact wasteland. But here existed the last of the secret places of amusement.

The theatres. Half a dozen of them, faceless but bristling with energy on the inside, full of make-believe and break-belief, with living actors and live music and deadpan ushers, pastel props and the magic of illusion, gateways to other worlds that were artificial but also intensely real, for their contrivance was perfectly integrated with the fabric of the world outside, pictures that enhanced the frames that gave them definition.

It was difficult to precisely explain the appeal.

In any system of chaos and fluctuation there will be pauses of indefinite length where order or even stagnation seems to be the rule, but this rule is just another arbitrary variation in the flux. The city had entered such a time of fake calm, of pseudo-structure, when the fires were lower, in hearts too, and all the loudest atavistic urges were sleeping soundly.

Myrrh asked, "Which theatre is it?"

"I'm not sure. It could be any of them, all of them perhaps. Maybe the play will be shared equally among them."

"I can't hear anything, no voices or music."

Gold strode towards the nearest building and glanced over his shoulder, as if to test her eyes with his receding grin, but she was capable of counting all his teeth at this distance and she followed recklessly, throwing back her head with a laugh that was a muted chomp on a rising glissando, one and half octaves in range. She joined him at the entrance.

They pushed open the ponderous doors together.

Inside the lobby there were shadows and litter, but the shadows had been neatly arranged as though tidied by a team of cleaners. The litter that made smaller shadows between the bigger shadows of the baroque pillars and rococo pargets was scattered randomly, but not alarmingly so.

Gold and Myrrh squinted at the low intensity bulbs.

"The lights might have been left on. They don't prove that anyone is here right now. Let's not get too excited."

"With respect, I was born excited and it's my nature."

"Then continue as you please."

"Shall we go into the auditorium? Circle or stalls?"

"A private box, I think..."

Up the broad stairs they swept, and the bulbs in niches of the walls were smaller and weaker the higher they went, but their eyes adjusted accordingly. At last they found the discreet red plush door that led to the most important box in the establishment and they passed through and emerged on an enclosed platform that was like a boat on a dark sea of contrivance.

They peered over the side, dangling hands in murk that

should have been wet but was dry. There were long tassels that hung down from the exterior of the box like seaweed ropes or jellyfish tentacles. The rows of seats below were curious coral reefs and perched on them were giant seahorses that shimmered in the currents of gloom and crepuscular light that flowed down the aisles, swirled over their heads, lapped the elevated stage.

Myrrh blinked beautifully at Gold and gestured.

"Are they real? Are they alive?"

"I don't know," he whispered back, "but if they are papier-mâché heads it's still an impressive and special sight."

One of the horse heads down below turned to look up at them, but it may have been a coincidence, a mindless motion of springs and oiled bearings rather than the deliberate movement of a sentient being.

The curtains began to open, noiselessly but with a solemnity that was so much louder than sound that Myrrh and Gold both winced slightly before their faces became blank servants of patience and mild anticipation. The horse heads were all facing the same way now, but one opened its wide jaws to receive the ice cream that a limb that might terminate in either a hand or a hoof – for it was too dark to be certain – lifted up to its mouth.

"Imagine biting instead of licking!" shivered Myrrh.

Gold chewed his lower lip.

The curtains had now drawn fully back and something was being lowered from the flies on cables. A man? But no, not quite, not at all. A torso, head and arms, or rather *many* human torsos, heads and arms, amalgamated into one. This was a variation on the upper half of a man, a diversification, some sort of weird fusion, interracial and ranging the full spectrum of athleticism and age. Young strong arms, flabby weak ones, ancient and sagging, at least two dozen of them, protruding at all angles from the chests, backs and stomachs, with a profusion of variable heads too, sprouting like hideous blooms from extra necks or directly out of patchwork flesh. And this descent into the proscenium had the casual and inexplicable horror of an undeserved nightmare.

At the same time a trap in the stage floor had slid open and the lower half of a man was rising up from the depths. But again, this lower part wasn't just a pair of legs and a pelvis. It was a herd of legs, a swarm of feet, as if photographs of a crazed dancer had been superimposed, a cluster of thighs and calves, a mob of shins and ankles. And the bare feet rapped their toes on the wooden boards of the platform it was planted on, which ascended smoothly until it was level with the stage and clicked into place. Then the other half descended precisely onto the gaping and sticky wound that was the summit of the grotesque waist and a horrible sucking noise confirmed that a tight seal had been made. The creature jerked, snapped open all its eyes, smiled at itself.

From the wings, left and right, came two wings on the ends of extendable rods. They were enormous, feathered like those of an angel but also ribbed like those of a bat. They slotted into position somewhere on the communal back of the abomination. The rods were retracted rapidly.

Gold and Myrrh strained to see what would happen next.

The creature tensed dramatically.

Then it began speaking. It uttered words from every mouth it possessed, all of them, and the result was cacophony. Different accents and tones, strident and gentle voices, high and booming, crooning and harsh, mocking and wistful. Some words were in languages unknown to Gold and Myrrh. Occasionally the mouths would seem to make sense, two or more of them would speak the same word at the same time, producing a choral effect.

But most of what followed was an indescribable babble.

And the monster made gestures.

It *acted*, performing many separate roles simultaneously.

Overlapping polyrhythmic theatre...

It flapped its enormous wings and flew in short hops around the stage but it was too heavy to soar over the audience.

Myrrh and Gold understood that here at last was a universal thespian, the conglomerated actor, manufactured from parts of all the human actors who had formerly inhabited and worked in this city, the sprawl known as Spittle, and that the idea and intention – *neither of which worked* – was to distil and concentrate the entire history of the art of the play into a single digestible experience. But it was beyond assimilation, outside appreciation, futile.

The audience began grumbling and this agitation and dissatisfaction made the storm of confused sound seem buoyed up on a drone, something substantial that threatened to sweep away the pandemonium and the multifaceted actor who generated it on a tide of vituperation, repel the being into the shadows at the rear of the stage, where abandoned props from other performances doubtless lurked like mantraps to cripple some of those limbs and heads. But the monstrosity on stage refused to sag under the onslaught. It acted harder. It moved and gestured, winced and blinked, chortled and wept, hammed it up to an extreme point where flesh itself seemed to be speaking and pleading.

The overworked mouths began to dribble, streams of saliva pouring over teeth or through the gaps between them, and the rate of flow increased and kept increasing, as if this absurd living thing, this experiment of some impresario and dabbler in dark science, was leaking and draining, spurting and spraying away at high pressure all the inner soup that gave it structure and definition. It might have deflated utterly, like a massively mutated bladder, had not the demands of the contradictory physical movements of the many roles tore it apart first. There was a ripping sound, the visible stretching and tearing of fibres, and one by one the arms fell off the shoulders. Then the ankles twisted and snapped, the necks broke, kneecaps rattled onto the stage, eyeballs popped out to roll around on the boards and be stamped flat by disintegrating feet.

But still the mouths drooled and now the saliva was pouring over the lip of the stage and into the auditorium, as if the stage itself was a huge mouth and the appalling actor inside it merely a confused and solidified jamming of words, the utterance of an overexcited prophet or lunatic, petrified by a malign alchemy that transformed not only sounds into things but also the echoes and overtones of those sounds. The horse heads snorted in alarm.

All at once the audience members had jumped up and were allowing pure panic to rule them, to guide their feet, which Gold and Myrrh now plainly saw weren't hooves at all. The heads were indeed false. Some crumpled in collision with each other, one or two even fell off to expose the frightened human visage beneath and mouths that poured drool of their own.

Leaning even further over the side of the box, Gold and Myrrh felt little surprise when the entire structure broke off from the wall and they plummeted down into the mêlée like two explorers in a bathtub going over a waterfall. The box landed upright with a violent shudder and they stood dazed and bruised as the tassels entangled themselves around the arms and necks of a dozen panicked audience members, who began bolting for the exit.

There was a stampede, a desperate flight away from the composite actor and his outpouring of drool, a scramble for the streets of Spittle, wet and oily in name alone, for the fresher but not fresh air, the higher but not high skies. Open burst the doors of the auditorium and through the lobby surged the crowd and Gold and Myrrh rode their chariot like reluctant warriors entering a conquered metropolis, bouncing and showering sparks on the surface of the uneven road as the frantic herd attempted to put as much distance between themselves and the theatre as feasible, dragging the box along behind them.

Horses peeled away from the main mass. Some tripped and remained on the ground or slowly stood and dusted themselves down before sauntering off in some other direction, removing their heads and slipping into the shadows. Now there were only the steeds that had become entangled in the tassels. Some of the tassels broke and the chariot slowed down. At last it came to a halt as those who still pulled it gave up the flight and sagged from fatigue.

Gold and Myrrh climbed out and began heading home, which was only a couple of streets away. They were shaken but still capable of post-play analysis and they discussed what they had seen all the way to their front door. Clearly it had been a big ironic joke: a chaotic play of all plays for a chaotic city, and yet the joke had backfired, because at the present time there was temporary order, stasis even, and Spittle was not a city of all cities but merely one variation in the interminable list of possible places. And the saliva had been a primitive device, spit without polish, a violation of all the drools.

"But the horses? What was that about?"

"We should have dressed up too. We weren't warned."

"Yes, but why? To see *that* play!"

"No one would have come if it had been advertised truthfully," Myrrh said thoughtfully. "Apart from you and me."

"Not even us," said Gold as they reached their house.

Before inserting the key, they kissed on the doorstep, exchanging saliva with tongues. The play hadn't finished yet.

The Mouth of Hell

On the evening of the Summer Solstice the brave explorers finally set off on the expedition that had been planned for so long by the university. When I say 'so long' I am referring to a subjective feeling they shared rather than any precise measurement of time. Anxiety had made the days seem long and unbearable but now the dramatic moment had arrived.

The longest day of the year had been chosen because there was less night and this was regarded as a comforting fact by most members of the team. Not that any moonlight would penetrate far into where they intended to delve. The date was purely of psychological benefit, for they were still human beings with the superstitious instincts of their ancestors.

I say 'they' but in fact I was also part of the expedition. However, my role was to stay behind and wait for their return, so I barely consider myself to have made a real contribution to the mission.

Collins, Fumble, Rigby, Lister, Ripple, Masson and Blister were their names. Seven heroes willing to risk everything in order to add just a little to the universal store of knowledge that belongs to us all. I admired them then and I admire them even more now. And I recall with acute feelings of bitter nostalgia the last sunset they ever saw as it reddened their faces in a cosmic blush on the steps of our university.

Then we walked slowly out of the town, and over the landscape, and soon the entrance of the mystery loomed ahead. This was the portal of fame or doom, depending on what destiny decided; but I do not believe in fate and it seemed of no great menace to me as I approached.

We stopped before it and made final preparations.

The idea had originally been to tether the explorers securely so they could be hauled back out in the event of an emergency but unmanned probes that had already been sent in indicated that ropes would snag on the superabundance of objects that crammed the enigmatic space.

None of the probes had returned, by the way, but they were designed for a one way trip, so this fact did not worry us.

Farewells were brief and every team member shook solemn hands with every other: Collins with Fumble, Rigby with Lister, Ripple with Masson, Blister with me, and so on. The explorers were equipped with food to last several months.

"Switch on your torches please!" cried Collins.

The group had no official leader but I guess someone had to give orders at certain points during that perilous mission. Beams of powerful, yet oddly unconvincing, light appeared to emanate from every hand and a complex mesh of insubstantial girders was suddenly created. Then the beams swivelled to point in one direction only, namely into the mouth of the anomaly.

"Good luck!" I called to them, wiping away a tear.

"Don't cry in public!" someone said.

I stiffened to attention but who was there to witness my dishonour? What shame is there in weeping anyway? My tears glinted very faintly in the starlight and only the moths knew anything. They fluttered past and tickled my ears and the powdery sensation of their wings on my lobes made me sob harder but with an unhealthy and involuntary mirth. And then—

They were gone. Not the moths but the explorers.

They had entered the object.

I did everything that was required of me. I sat on a portable camping chair and boiled milk for hot chocolate on a little gas stove. I twiddled my thumbs. In the morning I began reading the first of the books I had brought with me. That is how I passed the time. Every so often a university official would come to check but I never had anything to report.

No journalists ever arrived to interview me.

The story simply had no value for them at this stage. Only if the explorers returned blinking, arms loaded with mementoes, from that undoubtedly hellish region, would the press care about the mission. And they never came back out. That is the thing that needs to be stressed.

None of them ever emerged. The days and weeks became months and the months eventually joined hands into a year.

The funding ran out at that instant. I was required to stand up and fold the chair and take it back to the university. Everything felt heavy, especially a vague feeling of guilt I had, and I walked as if through molten lipstick, wearily and in despair of my shoes. The town seemed unfamiliar to me when I reached it and I entered the campus grounds like a stranger.

Collins, Fumble, Rigby, Lister, Ripple, Masson and Blister already were statues on the steps leading to the main entrance. Skilled masons had been busy in that year of etiolated ambitions. And I had a statue too, but it was of a pigeon with my face perched on the head of Collins, who somehow had posthumously acquired the status of leader. I shuddered.

Nothing was ever the same after that. I started drinking. Not to excess but to a lack of success, which is nearly as bad, and now I am here, in this bar, and you are the first journalist to care about my story. I know I met you by accident here, that you didn't seek me out, that we started talking randomly, but at least I have had a belated opportunity to tell the tale.

The journalist in question frowns and drains his brandy. His frown is imperfectly symmetrical. "A handbag!"

"Yes, that is correct."

"How extraordinary! Lost inside a handbag!"

"Indeed. It is terrible."

"They were your colleagues?"

"Yes and my friends."

"Were they little men? I mean, to fit inside a handbag they surely must be tiny figures as small as thumbs."

"They were of normal size. I knew them well."

"In that case, the handbag must have belonged to a giantess! Was it an enormous example of the type?"

"It was a perfectly ordinary handbag."

"I don't understand..."

"What is there to understand? It was a woman's handbag, no more or less, and they were men! And they will never return, never, and who knows what they are doing in there? Who outside can guess what inexplicable things they have found and are still finding? A *woman's* handbag! Now you must go away and leave me alone. I will say it one last time. They were ordinary sized men and the handbag was a typical handbag. They were men like me. That's all you need to know. The conversation is over."

He departs and I finish my whisky. Then I too get up and leave the bar and walk home along the dark streets.

And just in case the events of this true story seem no more than a jest based on chauvinism, let me put your mind at rest by declaring that before I reach my front door, both suspender buttons spontaneously pop and my black silk stockings slide down around my ankles.

The Strings of Segovia

It was a foggy night in Old London. Or perhaps it was the fog that was old, or just the night, or maybe only me, dressed as I was in antique garb. My jerkin and breeches were silken and rustled softly, my high boots and heavy gauntlets were leathern and squeaked pleasantly. As for my tricorne hat, I wore it with considerable aplomb. Even the sword that swung at my hip did not seem out of place. Only one item of clothing dissatisfied me and I wandered the streets in an attempt to remedy this defect.

Music emerged from the general fumy blur, the notes of a guitar carefully plucked, a haunting melody that evoked everything London was not. Although no words accompanied the playing I was reminded of balmy nights, iron balconies, dark women with flowers in their hair, the salty tang of olives, young wine. I am fond of street musicians. Indeed I am something of a patron to buskers and so I quickened my step toward the source of this acoustic magic. My present situation compelled me to engage the person responsible, but my motives were also partly altruistic.

I found a young man sitting in a doorway, his expression containing both the unquenchable hope of the compulsive dreamer and the feverish desperation of the chronically frustrated. He was poor, I noted at once, but not entirely without resources, strange reservoirs of inky self-belief. I loomed above him, listening quietly until his elegant song was concluded, then I reached into my pocket and deposited a handful of coins into the upturned cloth cap that gaped between his feet like the severed ear of a cyclops. His gratitude was a theatrical grin.

"You play extremely well — perhaps too well!" I announced.

He blinked at this compliment, and might have blushed into the bargain had not a tendril of cold fog suddenly turned the corner and tickled his face, discouraging all sunset cheeks, my own included. So he licked his lips instead and answered, "I have a good teacher."

"Oh?" I responded, retreating a pace, "and who might that be?"

He studied me closely, his gaze travelling from tricorne to spurs and back again, before glancing left and right like a storybook conspirator. "Segovia. None other."

I laughed: a short bark. "Come now!"

His voice was an urgent whisper. "It's true. I keep it a secret, to myself, because I don't care to be ridiculed but there's something about you I find reassuring, I don't know why. I trust you. Segovia really is my teacher. I've wanted to share this remarkable news with someone for many months but it was never possible until now. People would say I was mad. I imagine you are used to such comments, dressed the way you are. And so..."

"I am less eccentric than you think. I'm a man on a mission."

He frowned as if upset by my nonchalance and the fingers of his right hand rapped a sharp rhythm on the body of his guitar. "Do you believe me or not?"

"I don't, if that answer pleases you more..."

"Very well. I am due for my next lesson less than one hour from now. Come with me and see with your own eyes that Segovia is my teacher. My home isn't far. That's where we must go and it's polite and important to be on time. Are you willing?"

I rubbed my chin with the back of a gauntlet. "Certainly. Lead the way."

He stood and slung his instrument over his shoulder. Then he had vanished into the fog and it was no easy task to keep up with him and only the faint twang of strings in the currents of cold air betrayed his direction at each new corner. I steadily increased my pace, following these rogue harmonics, down countless streets and over several bridges, but only managed to reach his side after he paused in front of a door to wait for me.

While he fumbled with a key, I studied the building he had guided me to.

"This is your home?" I asked.

"Absolutely – in a manner of speaking!"

I ignored the contradiction and cried, "Segovia comes here:

to a house without windows?"

For an answer he unlocked the door and swung it open, stepping through rapidly and pulling me along with him. Then he was off again, and I was close on his heels, but no corridors or rooms did we pass through. Instead we rushed down more streets and turned more corners. I assumed I was still in London and that the door was some intact relic of ancient defences, a portal in a strong wall between two different quarters of the city, but slowly it became apparent that the simple crossing of the threshold had induced a profound change in the environment. For one thing, there was no fog here. None.

"This is not really your home," I declared.

"Wherever I learn my music, that's where my heart is. And where the heart is..."

I scowled furiously to prevent him from completing this maudlin utterance and then I slowed my pace to enable more careful scrutiny of my surroundings. He seemed irked by my tardiness but said nothing, following my gaze as I looked around, shifting his instrument to the other shoulder. *This* night was balmy and there were iron railings. Then a clock tower demonstrated that the time was one hour later than it should have been. When we turned another corner and a gigantic but curiously delicate aqueduct loomed before us, the truth could no longer be denied.

We were no longer in London, old or new.

"This is the city of Segovia – in Spain," I announced tonelessly.

He was mildly flustered but did not pause, leading me up a flight of stone steps at the side of the impressive structure. "Of course. What else did you expect? I told you Segovia was my teacher, I'm not a liar. Don't drag your feet now, we're almost there!"

I chuckled horribly. "I thought you were referring to Andrés Segovia, born in Linares in 1893, who learned to play on a guitar once owned by Paco de Lucena. He died in 1987, Segovia I mean, and was awarded a high title in his old age – the Marqués de Salobreña, I think it was – in return for his services to music. It was often claimed that he singlehandedly rescued the Spanish guitar from amateur gypsies, a view he shared himself. He remains one of the greatest guitarists of all time."

He gaped in bewilderment. "I don't know about any of that but it's critically important that I'm not late for my lesson. Segovia is my teacher, the city itself. That's a simple fact."

"I suppose the famous castle itself gives you lessons?" I mocked. "Or perhaps the church of Vera Cruz, built on mystic principles long ago by the Knights Templars?"

Now it was his turn to be annoyed. "Don't be ridiculous... Those structures wouldn't deal with a nobody like me. I'm just a commoner. My teacher is an ordinary house in a street leading off the Plaza Mayor. This way, please. Just a few more steps and then you'll see..."

And so I did. We had reached the great main square of the city, with the vast cathedral silhouetted against the stars, and now hurried down a narrow alley. Next to a closed restaurant stood a house with stone arms. It cradled the most enormous guitar in the world in its powerful and implausible hands and its upper stories seemed to hold an expression, although in no way did the design of the façade resemble a face. I was unable to resist making a wide sardonic bow but it ignored me utterly and concentrated all its attention on my companion. I was left with the impression that the windows blinked, though in fact they moved not at all and remained unlighted, mysterious.

"I'm here," the pupil called softly.

"Good," said the house, "and for this lesson we're going to focus mainly on chords and the execution of rapid but perfectly fluid key changes. We'll start as always with some scales, just to warm up the fingers. Are you ready? Take a deep breath and try to relax..."

I turned to leave, rubbing my jaw in consternation. The situation was too absurd. A house in Segovia that spoke English rather than Spanish? But I felt my sleeve plucked by an anxious hand and I was compelled out of politeness, the same politeness that matched my attire, formal and rigid but with a hint of lethal irony, to halt my departure and spend a few more minutes in conversation. My companion was very unhappy that he had to divide his concentration between myself and his teacher. He had already taken the urged deep breath and clearly did not want to expel it over me.

But finally he blabbered, "What's wrong?"

"I feel deceived," I explained simply.

"For what reason? I thought you wanted to listen to my lesson, hear my teacher play. I've never invited anyone else to accompany me here."

I arched an eyebrow. "I am returning to London. I will walk northwards for many weeks. You have wasted my time. Sir, your teacher is merely a house musician!"

He suddenly lunged forward and clapped his palm over my mouth, heedless of the sword I wore and the personality that made using such a weapon perfectly feasible and even easy. Protecting his teacher from further insult was more important to him than life itself. His words tumbled out for now he was desperate to be rid of me and become a single unit with his guitar. His compassion was the fastest I have ever witnessed.

"Fair enough, if you truly feel like that, but you are mistaken, horribly so. Don't return to London the long way, the real geographical route. Retrace our steps and pass back through the door. Close it behind you to stop the fog coming in. You wear your antique clothes with style, all expect one item. Farewell and good luck. One day you may regret your decision. Segovia plays like an angel, a stone angel. I love my teacher and believe my feelings are reciprocated, even though there is a small kitchen instead of a heart inside its dubious analogue of a chest. Furthermore..."

I stepped back and liberated my lips. "I have no intention of looking for that magic portal. I want nothing more to do with you. I will take the old route home."

And I stamped off. Northwards. But the moment I knew I was out of sight I doubled back and headed south down a different street. I couldn't hear the music of that absurdly vast guitar but I felt the vibrations of its strings, each as thick as a swollen thumb, a thumb accidentally bruised by a slammed front door or falling window, in my stained soul. Those spiritual chords would have been pleasant had a less rascally man experienced them. I shrugged. When I turned the next corner I encountered a young man with an easel and brushes.

"You paint extremely well – perhaps too well!" I announced.

He blinked at this compliment, gazing at me while I gazed at his work, the bright points of primary colour on the canvas seeming to glow, the details soft and yet unmistakable in a scene that was highly unrealistic and yet fixed perfectly the mood it was intended to capture. I waited for him to blush or speak.

"Who is your teacher?" I prompted.

Roused from his daze he responded forcefully, "Liechtenstein. None other."

I sighed and shook my head. "You aren't referring to Roy Lichtenstein, the artist famous for adapting the techniques of comic book illustration, are you? He was born in 1923 and died in 1997. I suspect you mean the nation of Liechtenstein, the only double-landlocked country in Europe, meaning it is entirely surrounded by other landlocked countries. My guess is that an ordinary house in a normal street is your teacher, a house with stone arms and a gigantic paintbrush clutched in its brick hands."

"Yes, and my next lesson takes place in one hour..."

I continued to shake my head. "Wrong direction," I explained. "I don't go north or east but due south, a long way. Indeed my journey has scarcely begun. My destination is the most southerly great city of Africa. I'll hop through as many magic doors as possible to get there but yours is no use to me. When no doors are available I'll walk or hitch. London to Segovia was only the first stage. I travel to attend my first lesson from my own teacher."

He was at a loss for appropriate words. "The capital of Liechtenstein is Vaduz."

"Yes I know. Farewell. Good luck."

"Thank you," he stammered but his lips stopped quivering when I answered sharply. "I was talking to myself!" Then I was gone, my high boots clicking on the cobbles. What lesson did I hope to learn in that particular place, far below the equator? My jerkin and breeches rustled softly. My gauntlets, hat and sword acted in exactly the way that suited me best. Only my cape gave me trouble. And there, on the tip of that mighty continent, where two oceans collided, from a city most wise in such matters, from Cape Town itself, I knew I would receive instructions on how to wear it properly.

Paired Down

There is a curious shop in a street near my house. Only once have I visited it and I went inside just to learn what it sold, because I passed it every day on my way to work and there was nothing on display in the window to give a clue, and inside me grew a powerful desire to know.

The sign under the iron bracket that jutted from the wall was so weathered and faded and grimy it couldn't be read and that was the most frustrating thing of all. What if something I truly wanted was waiting for me behind the counter? This question was one I asked myself in a sort of rhetorical fashion, for I am not a materialistic person and never expected to actually cross the threshold and play the role of customer.

But my job was unsatisfactory and the walk to my office became more and more agreeable than the actual arrival and it was inevitable I would try to prolong my journey; one morning I found myself pushing open the door.

"Just browsing," I said to the shopkeeper as soon as the little bell chimed. Then I realised the room was completely bare.

The shopkeeper rubbed his hands together and stepped out of the shadows, a thin man with watery blue eyes and a yellow beard. He shook his head. "It is not permitted to inspect the merchandise before buying."

"How eccentric!" I exclaimed.

He fixed me with a suspicious stare. "Is this your first time in a *Done Things Differently* store?"

To which I gave an airy wave. "Of course not."

He clucked his tongue. "Your answer proves that it is. Nobody ever comes in here twice. Only one purchase is allowed, there are no refunds and no possibilities of an exchange. Do I make myself clear?"

"In a vague and misty way, yes."

"The price is different for everybody and the tariff is set according to my perception of a customer's needs. First I will examine you from a distance and then whisper the exact sum in your ear."

He did so and I twitched. "That is a considerable amount."

He shrugged and retreated back into the shadows. It was only at this point that I noticed another figure in the shop, a man standing in a narrow alcove who was counting the money in his wallet with trembling fingers. When he was satisfied he had the required quantity of high denomination notes he emerged rather sheepishly and passed them to the shopkeeper who pocketed all with a motion so lizardlike that I expected him to flicker a forked tongue.

He seemed to read my thoughts. "This isn't one of those fantastical stories written by lazy authors who always favour a cliché over an original image. I am no less human than yourself. And I'm not particularly sinister."

"What shall I call you?" I asked.

"Idris Gecko. The surname is just a coincidence. This shop has been in my family for generations and is passed down from father to son in a ceremony of our own devising. We offer a unique service to those who are unhappy with the state of their lives, the opportunity to correct a single past mistake, and that is the only thing on sale here. Are you tempted?"

"I'm not sure," I replied.

Before I could say more, the other customer walked towards a curtain at the back of the room and passed through it. I wanted to see what was on the other side but the shopkeeper blocked my path. "You must meet my price first. Haven't I already explained the procedure to you?"

"But I still don't understand what I'll be paying for."

"Did you wander in off the street? Well that occasionally happens, though most of my clients learn of this place through word of mouth. I can resolve the mystery for you easily enough. Our lives are full of decisions, big and small. Whenever we face a decision, we create two potential futures, two branches on the river of time, and some of these branches are thicker than others. The two thickest can be found at the point where we have to make the most crucial decision of our lives. Often we aren't aware of the significance of that decision at the time and can't identify the precise moment it was forced on us."

"True. All we can do is accept the consequences."

"Not so!" He clapped his hands. "I can show you what sort of a man you would have become if you had followed the other branch. Consider those decisions that have faced you: shall I apply for this job? Shall I ask that girl to marry me? Shall I buy this house or that one? The list of crucial decisions is enormous. Whatever was the most important decision you made, and it's different for everyone, it will have created a parallel version of yourself, potentially a happier and more successful man. I can introduce you to that man, your other self, in the room adjacent to this one. You can meet him and he can help you, give you advice, become your mentor, help you improve your situation."

I frowned and asked, "I regret several decisions made when I was younger. May I pick one of those to alter?"

"The short answer is no. Only the most important decision of your life can be changed, and it might not be on your list of regrets. Indeed in my experience a man rarely can pinpoint it accurately on his lifestream. So accepting the services of my shop is an act of blind faith."

"Certainly, but there is no risk attached?"

"I'm opposed to answering that question. However, before you decide to strike a deal, I must be more specific as to the nature of your purchase. Suppose the most important decision of your life occurred at a moment ten years ago. In this case, the man waiting for you behind that curtain has had an entire decade to develop along his different branch. He will be very wise, very capable, and the help he can offer will be considerable. But if the most important decision of your life occurred only last week, then your alternative self won't have had much time to evolve and can't be much different from you. His assistance will probably be of minimal use and the transaction will be poor value."

I opened my mouth to speak but my words were forestalled by a bustle on the far side of the curtain. The customer who had preceded me emerged with a man who might have been his twin brother, a more successful brother, a fellow who looked almost the same but had healthier skin, a brighter twinkle in the eyes, an air of greater maturity and confidence and style. They hurried out of the shop without a glance at myself or the shopkeeper.

"Another satisfied customer," said Idris Gecko.

Impulsively I made my decision. "Here is my money! Take it quickly! All of it! Hurry! Why the unbearable delay?"

The shopkeeper arched a sceptical eyebrow at me. Then I remembered to actually take the notes out of my wallet and pass them to him. He crumpled them in a hand held close to his flaking ear, savouring the crispness and its constriction, then opening his palm and letting the valuable oblongs unfurl, his smile both childish and wise.

"You won't regret this – or perhaps you might," he said.

"I want to be paired with a more successful version of myself, so he can guide me towards a brighter future," I declared. "For him the arrangement might not be so useful but what do I care?"

Idris Gecko bowed low. "In that case, pass through the curtain!"

I hurried forward at once, like a bull at a cape, my horns the thick throbs of anticipation in my temples. The curtain fabric was coarse, and I didn't enjoy the way it felt on the skin of my face, but within moments I was on the other side, blinking the dust out of my eyes. To my disappointment it seemed I had simply rotated on the spot, for ahead of me was the same shop interior with the same door at the far end. But the shopkeeper had vanished. Where was my superior double?

I wondered if I should call for him but to call yourself by your own name feels a little pretentious, especially when an answer is not guaranteed. Thus I delayed... Then I saw a dark figure pass the window, a man clearly on his way to work, hurrying because he was late. I recognised myself at once and called anxiously: "Dear me, please wait for me!"

But he had already gone and I realised that to chase after him was my only option. I crossed the floor of the empty shop, flung open the door and jumped into the street. Then I pounded the paving slabs with feet unaccustomed to such ordeals as running. He was in a rush but eventually I caught up with him and rested my hand on his shoulder.

"Why are you bothering me?" he demanded.

"The teacher and the pupil must be formally introduced," I

gasped.

He blinked and his features softened. "Remarkable! You look like a more successful version of me, with healthier skin, a brighter twinkle in the eyes, an air of greater maturity and confidence and style... Not much more successful, granted, but a little. Perhaps enough."

"No, no! It's the other way around!"

"And you have come to act as my guide? To improve my drab life?"

"There has been a mistake!" I wailed.

Then I knew that Idris Gecko had tricked me, or rather had allowed me to deceive myself. Always we are too quick and eager to blame ourselves, to demean the choices we have made, imagine we are never the best we could be. But at that moment the other truth was plain. When the most crucial decision of my life was taken, I had made the right choice, after all. My alternative self was the one who had chosen badly...

And now I was stuck with him. His teacher.

I didn't want the role but he linked his arm in mine and I had to work in the same office as he so it was easier to fall into step. He badgered me for good advice on a host of problems and I stuttered my replies. I wasn't much wiser than he, just a little, a little that I didn't believe was enough, but I had no heart to voice my doubts on this score.

The worst part of the ironic situation was this: my most crucial life decision had been whether to enter that shop or not. Only that. I had made the correct decision, entering and giving the shopkeeper my money. My odd twin had not. It was laughably anticlimactic. How much time had I been given to develop significantly along my own branch? No more than ten minutes. The result? A worthless guide, an accidental charlatan.

As Idris Gecko declared, this isn't one of those fantastical stories written by a lazy author who always favours a cliché over an original image, and yet the next time I walked down that street the shop had gone. In its place was merely an area of rubble, urban wasteland waiting for redevelopment, a patch of nowhere, a cavity in the urban grimace.

Maybe the street is not really the same. It occurs to me that

I passed right through the building, rather than entering and leaving at the same point. The two parallel worlds don't overlap exactly. I have displaced my existence by the length of one shop or the distance of one universe. None of this bothers my pupil. His devotion and questions are relentless.

We work at the same bland desk, legs jammed uncomfortably together in our small cubicle. Narcissism will never be possible for me now. Strange that a man should come to bitterly regret making the right choice when faced with the most important decision of his life. I dream of wrong choices, lusting for them palpably. Somehow this paradox must be beneficial for me. That is my condition. I have been paired down.

Arms Against a Sea

I found an arm washed up on the beach, not a real arm but a carved one, a marble block chiselled into the shape of a slender female limb. It emerged from the midnight waves like the final gesture of a drowned swimmer, its pale fingers digging into the sand, a loop of seaweed around its wrist for a bracelet, its elbow jabbing a moonbeam.

I hurried through the surf to rescue the arm but the moment I picked it up I couldn't be sure who was the *holder*, who the *held*. That is always the way with castaway arms so I used it as a crutch to help me back to shore, and when I reached my house in the hills I planted it in the bucket where I keep my umbrellas. Then I went to bed.

In the morning I puzzled over my unusual find but could make neither head nor tail of it, which was appropriate enough, and so I packed it in an empty quiver and cycled with it slung over my shoulder to the library. My simple request confused the librarian on duty and she frowned for several minutes. "A reference book about arms!"

"Yes please, do you have such a volume I may consult?"

"You mean weapons?" she asked.

"No. I mean proper arms, good old-fashioned upper limbs. I found one last night I want to identify, you see."

"Do you happen to have it with you?" she muttered.

"In this quiver here. Allow me…"

I laid the arm on the counter and she blinked through her spectacles at it with growing astonishment. Then she stroked it with a finger, shook her head, breathed heavily, and cried:

"The lost right arm of the Venus de Milo!"

"Are you sure?" I blurted.

She nodded. "Absolutely certain. This is an astonishing discovery! We must notify the Louvre at once!"

And she tried to snatch the arm and pull it completely over her side of the counter but I was too fast and soon an unseemly tug of war began, an aggressive tussle in which I had the distinct impression the arm itself was trying to aid my efforts. Needless to say, I won and returned the object to my quiver with a magnificent scowl.

"I can't allow it to be sent to Paris on its own. It must be reunited with its twin, the lost left arm. My mission is to find that other arm. Only then may the authorities be contacted."

"The project is unfeasible!" she snarled.

But I refused to be dissuaded so easily and I ran out of the library and mounted my bicycle. I had no particular destination in mind but with only a little pondering I surmised that the best place to seek the other arm was on the far side of the world, on the beach antipodal to my own, for clearly the arms had been trying to embrace the entire planet, snapping off as the consequence of such an ambitious hug.

That hypothesis kept me going through cold rain and the humid steam of dense tropical jungles, over the peaks of snowy mountains and into the greedy ooze of swamp and marsh. I slept always with her firm arm below my pillow, in fact her arm *was* my pillow, but I often drew her out of the quiver to help me pick fruit from tall trees.

Sometimes she scratched my back, dug trenches…

It's not really possible to fall in love with a woman who isn't there, and I can't honestly say I regarded the Venus de Milo as my girlfriend, or even as a dominatrix I yearned to serve, but there was a connection between us stronger than academic interest. Maybe I regarded her as the embodiment of an ideal synthesis between purity and lust.

After many years of travelling I reached a tiny unnamed island along a causeway whose flints finally ruptured my tyres. With regret I abandoned my bicycle, stumbled onwards to the beach that was directly opposite my original home on the surface of the globe and there, in the sparkling surf, I beheld the sleek white object of my desire.

Over the rocks I scrambled, stubbing my toes. But disappointment was waiting for me among the starfish.

"A bone! A marble bone! I am too late!"

This arm had been eroded until all its stony flesh had fallen off, all its mineral nerves and veins had unravelled, leaving only the relevant part of the sculpted skeleton, a work of exquisite art by itself, true, but a fetish of grief also, and I preferred not to hold it for too long before hurling it back to the very waves that had gnawed upon it.

Then I wondered if only beaches have antipodal equivalents, so I went to locate the inverse of my house, and also its owner, my own reciprocal, and I found both in place in the low hills. In the twilight I used her good arm to rap on the door and to my astonishment it was opened from inside by her other good arm. I sank to my knees.

"Don't be hasty with your ecstasy," cautioned a voice.

"It's not a miracle?" I blinked.

He shook his head, a bearded man with dust in his wrinkles, and I saw that he was wearing her left arm as a prosthetic limb, having lost his own in an industrial accident or an explosion. Then he explained that the bone had been removed to make this false arm lighter, more usable, and that he was perfectly satisfied with the result.

Something about this wasn't logical. "But how could you perform such a delicate operation with only one arm?"

"The extraction of the bone and fitting of the limb were included in the price," he said, "and required no effort from me. Take further questions to the curio shop where I purchased it."

Then he closed the door in my face. I had wanted to ask the way to the curio shop but obviously that was one of the so-called further questions I had to ask at the curio shop itself. Maybe I could locate the information at the local library? If everything truly had its antipodal equivalent here, that musty building should be no exception.

I proceeded down a curving road, turned the final bend and to my mild surprise discovered the curio shop in the place I had calculated the library would be. Not all equivalences are exact, not all reciprocals symmetrical. I pushed my way inside and lost myself among the leftovers of a hundred thousand cultures, valid and imaginary.

The curio shop seemed to contain for real all those things described by all the books in my library. A close enough mirror image, possibly even a superior reflection. I negotiated the unique maze and reached the counter after a long struggle. The shopkeeper rapped his fingernails on the dented surface while I rummaged in my quiver.

I withdrew the arm, laid it down. "It's no longer special to me and so I must sell it. How much is it worth?

"Plenty, but we don't buy things here, my friend."

"Will you swap a curio for it?"

He pensively stroked the marble wrist. "Perhaps I can convert it into an artificial Zen applauder, or something along those lines, as the Venus de Milo herself has no resonance for me. But wouldn't you regard that as a violation of your ultimate woman?"

I tugged my beard and dust trickled from the wrinkles in my face as I frowned at the arm. "It's quite useless without the left limb, for my dream of being fully embraced is ruptured."

"But how does *she* feel about it?" he wondered.

"She's not my girlfriend yet," I said.

With a sigh, he turned and mounted a ladder to a high shelf. "I think I have a solution that will satisfy both of us," he remarked, as he selected a murky glass phial from the shadows.

I studied the swirl of the liquid inside and pocketed the phial carefully after he explained that it was a potion that encouraged broken statues to regrow their missing parts. But they would regrow those parts differently according to updated circumstances. "If the context has changed, the new growth will adapt to it," he pointed out.

This news filled me with delight. It was imperative I reach Paris with my treasure rapidly and smear it over the stumps of my cold darling. Her limbs would sprout with the force of long repressed passion and entwine my torso like the branches of a fig tree, clasping me tightly to her perfect bosom, to her classic bounty, forever.

I trudged narrow paths, forded broad rivers...

In the Louvre I finally stood before her and secretly applied the lotion, but the desired effect wasn't instantaneous. How could it be? I knew that lustful impatience had distorted my reason and so I resolved to return the following week. When the fateful day arrived I smartened myself as best I could and walked into her presence.

But the spectacle that greeted me was both awful and inevitable. Too many centuries adrift in the ocean at the mercy of currents, dragged along the seabed over reefs, battered by the breakers of wild shores, alone with crustaceans, had wrought their alchemy. Even statues will evolve to meet the demands of a fresh environment.

While ghoulish tourists flocked to take photographs and guards vainly attempted to push them back, I passed blandly through the mob and stood directly before her, gazing up sadly, unflinching. Then I laughed. In place of the smooth enticing arms of a beautiful goddess were now the upraised menacing claws of a gargantuan crab.

The Martian Monocles

It's true: we know more about the surface of Mars than the bottom of the ocean, but not for want of trying. The problem with diving so deep is that the pressure is enormous and only the strongest bathyspheres can survive a journey right down to the abyssal plain. Many vessels and explorers have been crushed over the years attempting to plumb the ultimate limits of the deepest marine trenches.

Every time a bathysphere implodes somewhere far under the seas of Earth, the most advanced beings on Mars shed big oily tears in sympathy, but not because they assign a high value to human life. No. They aren't even aware that those bathyspheres are crewed. Such misunderstandings are normal between the life forms of different worlds and only rarely can an authentic connection be made.

The Martians in question resemble giant eyeballs that have fallen out of colossal heads and a legend says that when they all weep together the ancient dry riverbeds of the red planet fill to the brim with doleful water, but, in fact, there aren't enough of them to produce sufficient liquid for that. What *is* true is that the eyelids that slam like shutters to protect them are the same colour as the desert.

These eyeball beings are clairvoyant and that's how they know about the bathyspheres on Earth. They see images in their minds that are almost as clear as the pictures they focus on for real. They dislike being stared at and are instantly aware when anyone or anything tries to study them from afar, and that's why it took so long to detect them. They aren't exactly shy but they do value their privacy.

The moment a telescope is trained on them or a probe passes overhead the eyelids close and they remain very still, so nothing can be seen but the endless desert with its scattering of spherical rocks. When the intruder has gone, the rocks turn back into eyeballs. They move by rolling and they derive nourishment purely from photons. In other words they eat whatever they see, just like fat men.

It was only by accident that humans first made contact with

them and the circumstances of that encounter are so unlikely they are worth telling again. A habitual sleepwalker on one of the first exploratory missions got out of his hammock in the middle of the night, suited up inside his rocket, opened the airlock and walked off alone. He was still fast asleep when he blundered into a group of eyeballs.

Because his eyes were closed all the time, and his conscious mind was switched off, the Martians didn't telepathically pick up his vibrations or take evasive action until it was too late. The astronaut woke up as soon as he hit the ground and then it was pointless for the eyeballs to pretend they still didn't exist. So Mars and Earth were introduced to each other. Formal trade links were rapidly established.

Unfortunately, it turned out that the Martians had nothing the humans wanted, and the humans only had one resource the eyeballs valued at all. Books. To be precise, the books of one author: Ray Bradbury. Try as they might, the humans couldn't interest the Martians in any other writer, not even Isaac Asimov, Frank Herbert or Kim Stanley Robinson. So crates of Bradbury titles were rocketed to Mars.

As those rockets took off from the launch pads of Earth, the heat of the departing exhausts turned winter days into summer, melting snowdrifts and baking nostalgic cakes in ovens not yet lit. But that doesn't concern us now. Every Bradbury volume was reprinted and small-press magazines from the 1940s were trawled in an effort to retrieve those numerous short stories that the author had disowned.

The Martians devoured these works but, because the eyeballs were so big and the typeface in the books so small in comparison, severe eyestrain was the inevitable result. Soon every Martian was myopic. They bumped into each other constantly as they trundled over the desiccated continents and irritation turned to anger, then anger became a desire for revenge. An interplanetary incident was inevitable.

Disaster was averted by the resourceful owner of a spectacle shop who recalled an old fable about a Spanish lens grinder who made an enormous monocle for a cyclops. This was lucky, as nobody else seemed to know that story. He saw no reason why the spectacle factories of Earth couldn't make monocles for the Martian market. His idea was taken up by various governments and rapidly implemented.

Soon the eyeballs could see clearly again and the wearing of monocles even imparted to them an aristocratic air they hadn't possessed before and the reissuing of the entire Ray Bradbury back-catalogue was resumed and everything should have been fine but a new problem arose in the wake of the solution. That's often the way. While wearing their massive monocles, the Martians were no longer able to roll.

An eyeball is a spheroid and spheroids move like balls, but a monocle is a disc and its flat surface impedes that kind of motion. Anger became a desire for revenge again. A second interplanetary incident loomed and it seemed that two worlds would be forced to engage in mutual destruction with futuristic rays because of a retrogeneric Ray, which sounds neat but isn't. All because of short sightedness!

Fortunately, the owner of the spectacle shop was also a transportation expert. Neat coincidence that. He quickly grasped that the dry riverbeds of Mars could be utilised as roads, as twisting freeways that would enable joined eyeballs facing away from each other to employ their monocles as wheels, eating up the Martian kilometres on the transparent rims of those vision rectifiers. An ingenious solution.

Although the Martians were loose eyeballs and hadn't lived in sockets for aeons they still possessed residual optic nerves that dangled like short tails from behind, just as the coccyx of humans is a residual tail. A pair of friendly Martians could splice these nerves into a flexible but strong axle, and that's what they did, rapidly acquiring a taste for high speed cruising and irresponsible driving while blinking.

The owner of the spectacle shop had become an unofficial ambassador to the red planet and he warned the drivers to take more care, to cut their speed, to keep their eyes on the road, but the third part of that advice was a joke because no matter how inept they were they couldn't do otherwise, and soon enough there was carnage everywhere and a third interplanetary incident was on the verge of erupting…

At this point the owner of the spectacle shop gave up. He couldn't be bothered to avert another apocalyptic war. It was somebody else's turn. He concentrated on relocating his entire stock into a subterranean bunker and living in close confinement with many wives. History doesn't record his name, partly because history no longer exists, but rumour maintains it was Yrubdarb Yar. Sounds foreign to me.

It just remains to explain the significance of the Martian empathy for bathyspheres. They think that bathyspheres are the true dominant form of life on Earth because of their shape, so when they implode under the sea and a perfectly round bubble of gas escapes and breaks the surface, the Martians believe they are observing a soul leaving its physical body and ascending to the realm of eyeball ghosts.

Suddenly

Suddenly, I was confronted by Cirle, the low albedo albino, who entered my house through an open window. Suddenly, he demanded a cup of tea, so I went to the kitchen to boil a kettle. Suddenly, he changed his peculiar mind and asked for coffee instead and I was happy to oblige and, when I took it to him, he drank it down in one gulp, burning his throat without a murmur of discomfort, like an overflow.

Suddenly, he leaned closer and said, "Did I ever tell you about a man I met a month ago who is known as the Maltese Hunter S. Thompson? He practices Gozo journalism, that's why!"

Suddenly, I felt apprehensive. Suddenly, I realised that Cirle was in one of his funny moods and that it would be difficult to get rid of him, to have a peaceful evening by myself. Suddenly.

Suddenly, he suggested that we catch a bus to London, to go and see a West End shah, (not the same thing as a West End show). Suddenly, I found myself nodding and leaving my warm house and travelling to the big, cold city, even though I didn't want to, and buying tickets for the theatre and going inside and sitting down on a folding seat.

Suddenly, midway through the performance, Cirle shouted at the top of his high voice, "What shah is this anyway?" and the answer came back from an unseen spectator, "Abbas! It's Shah Abbas, one of the greatest of shahs! Be silent and show some respect!"

Suddenly, I knew I wanted to leave, to find another form of amusement or lose Cirle and make my way back home alone. Suddenly, I felt a nudge in my ribs and understood that Cirle was bored with what was unfolding on the stage, which was just a figure in robes and turban talking about his conquests in the 17th Century, nothing more. Suddenly, Cirle stood up and stormed out, dragging me along with him.

Suddenly, as the cold night air hit me in the face, I wanted to be back inside the theatre, in the warm, away from this thin pallid demonic friend who unnerved me to such an enormous extent. Suddenly, he hailed a taxi and bundled me inside when it stopped.

Suddenly, he winked slyly at me and instructed the driver to take us to the nearest airport and I wanted to protest but I felt paralysed by the grim atmosphere of the unfolding vista through the windows. Suddenly, I knew that I would never see my home again.

Suddenly, we arrived at the airport and Cirle pushed me out of the taxi and we went to buy tickets for the most unlikely available destination and I felt feeble beneath his thin but hugely powerful grip on my shoulder; and I wondered where all my willpower had gone, my ability to assert myself, to strive against coercion, and I concluded that it had travelled on ahead of me and that I would catch it up in Iran.

Suddenly, I found myself on the aeroplane destined for Iran and sitting next to Cirle, who muttered into my right ear, "I'll be a shah greater than Abbas, mark my words!" and I marked them carefully and he got six out of ten, a comfortable pass, if not a merit.

Suddenly, I understood part of his dastardly plan but before I had the opportunity to attempt to reason with him and talk him out of it, one of the flight attendants came down the aisle towards us and said in a friendly but firm voice, "Excuse me, gentlemen, but don't you know that the word 'suddenly' should never be used in a work of fiction: it's one of the main rules of truly great creative writing."

Suddenly, I found myself answering her back with, "What may we use as a substitute then? Is 'abruptly' acceptable?" and she nodded with a thin smile and turned to deal with some other passengers and Cirle grumbled and refused to reflect much light despite the fact he was an albino and we landed in Iran and had lots of adventures.

Suddenly, more things happened and, suddenly, I realised I didn't want to describe them and, suddenly, I regretted starting this tale, which after all is only a mockery of something that doesn't really matter, as pale a satire as the colour of normal albinos in real life or other fiction, and no sooner had I resolved to stop writing it than—

Abruptly, nothing sudden happened!

Stand and Deliver

When Grub the postman finished his morning shift he usually had enough time to head out of town for a tankard of special ale before going back to work. There was an isolated tavern in a forest clearing that served the best food and drink he had ever experienced.

He didn't bother returning his sack of mail to the depot. It would save valuable minutes if he simply took it with him. So he stood by the side of the road and waited for a carriage. The quaint, retrograde nature of life in the Duchy of Klipklop still amazed him.

A far cry from his former existence in England, in the city of Coventry where he was daily abused on his rounds! Immigrating to this arcane state in an almost forgotten corner of Europe was the best decision he had ever made. He still believed that he was clever.

A carriage arrived and Grub climbed into it. There were no cars, or any other forms of motorised machinery in Klipklop, no internal combustion engines at all. Horses did the work. And women. And postmen. Everyone else sat around smoking pipes or grinning.

He was the only passenger today and he sank deeply into the padded seat. He knew this carriage would drop him near the doors of the isolated tavern and that another carriage coming the other way would convey him back to town approximately one hour later.

The carriage turned a bend and came to a sudden halt. A man blocked the road with a menacing smile, a sinister cape and mask, and a pistol that was aimed at the driver. This man approached closer, quickly opened the door and bowed rather mockingly at Grub.

"Stand and deliver!" he cried.

"But it's my lunchtime. Can't you come back later?"

The pistol was cocked. "No."

Grub sighed. "Very well. If I have to do one or the other, I'll deliver. I doubt I'm permitted to do both, as the regulations of the Postal Workers' Union are very strict. I'll be certain to lodge a complaint with them about this outrage. It's my free period!"

And he jumped down from the carriage and began walking back along the road towards the town, shifting his mail sack from one shoulder to the other as he went. The highwayman was too flabbergasted to discharge his gun at him and merely watched him go.

Grub sighed and grumbled and cursed as he reached the town and then he proceeded to deliver all the remaining letters in his sack. He went up a granite stairway and down a twisting cobbled alley. Finally, he had to stop in front of a tall blue house and ring the bell.

A man opened the door and blinked at Grub who blinked back. "I have a parcel for you," said Grub. "It's too big to slide under your door. In fact it's the biggest parcel I've ever carried."

"Thanks. The afternoon mail is very early today!"

"I was ordered by a highwayman to deliver it now, that's why. You'll have to sign here if you want the parcel."

The man signed a receipt and then took the box that Grub passed him and staggered under its weight. "It's very heavy! I wonder what it can be?" He set it down gently on the ground.

"None of that is my business," pointed out Grub.

"True," said the man, "but I'm going to open it in front of you anyway. I have been known to open parcels in front of postmen before. My name is Jagger, incidentally. I don't mean that 'incidentally' is my surname, so don't labour under that misapprehension!"

"I only labour under the discretion of my rightful employers," insisted Grub, as Jagger tore open the box. No sooner had he ripped off the paper covering and untied the string holding the box shut than something inside jumped out. It was the highwayman from before!

The miscreant bowed ironically. "I guessed you might try a trick like this, so I wrapped myself as a parcel and persuaded an actor to work as a decoy on the road. I'm glad my scheme and foresight have proved to be correct. So I'll say it again: stand and deliver!"

Grub rolled his eyes. "Do I really have to?"

Jagger whimpered, "But he's Swishing Shoehorn, the most infamous and depraved bandit in Klipklop! Do everything he says if you want to remain alive. He has been known to eat spoons!"

"I eat them with a knife and fork, I'm not a savage!" pointed out the rascal with a menacing scowl. "And I make those items of cutlery from frozen soup shaped in special moulds!"

"Very well," conceded Grub, "I'll stand this time. The Postal Workers' Union will be furious if I deliver twice."

And before Swishing Shoehorn could explain his meaning properly, Grub had already reached down and removed the bicycle clips from his own legs. It was only at this point that the highwayman realised that Grub wasn't a normal Klipklop citizen. Jagger was also amazed. Without any warning, Grub quickly rose into the sky.

"His legs are immensely long!" gasped Jagger.

Swishing Shoehorn removed his tricorne hat and scratched his wig with his pistol barrel. "He kept them doubled up all this time and has been walking around on his knees..."

"Doubled up? Tripled up, more like! Quadrupled up!"

But, in fact, Grub's legs were folded no less than seventeen times. With the absence of the clips holding the separate folds together he was free to stand up properly for the first time in years. His weird multi-jointed legs were the prime reason he had decided to leave Coventry and emigrate to Klipklop. They attracted too much attention.

Like a concertina they expanded, those legs, taking him higher. Then he hit his head on the underside of a cloud. The sky above Klipklop was solid but this fact didn't alarm him for he knew that the Duchy existed far below the nation of Liechtenstein. There simply wasn't space on the surface. Europe was already too crowded...

There was a trapdoor in the cloud and the handle was on the outside, so he turned it and his head passed through the sky to the other side, emerging in the throne room of a castle or palace.

The Duke of Klipklop, a man who delighted in the name Fig the Date, was yawning loudly. The room was full of jesters, all of them dressed in motley, walking on their hands, shaking rattles or posing annoying riddles that were instantly solvable. "I've been sentenced but I'm no criminal. What am I? A paragraph! I'm shaped like a spiral but there's nothing beyond me. What am I? A twist ending! I can be drawn but there's no…"

"An outline. You're an outline!" shrieked the Duke.

The jesters continued to caper and play.

The Duke sighed, "If only my court was like courts in the upper world, with a thousand serious fellows for every jester, but down here it's the other way around and I'm only allowed one straight man. And *he* died of pleurisy last week. Now he's gone I don't have any reason to remain sane. I wish I could find his replacement!"

Suddenly he noticed Grub's head and its demoralised expression rising through the floor in the middle of the room.

The Duke pointed at it in gratitude.

"You'll do," he said.

Trophy Wife

Word soon spread that Hubert had found himself a trophy wife. So there were three in the village now, if the story was true, which it might not be, and Dorian doubted it. "He doesn't have the capacity to acquire one; that is a fact, not an insult," he said to Gregor.

But it was an insult and they both knew it, a justified insult, for Hubert had never been remotely attractive to the opposite sex, neither in physical nor financial terms. And as for his personality: it was fungal and squalid, useful only for repulsing vermin and bats.

"But it could be worthwhile checking, just to be sure," replied Gregor, and he raised his head to gaze up the hill at the modest mansion that stood there, misshapen, almost deflated, crumbling, flaking, completely out of place in these environs, a true abomination.

Dorian considered this suggestion and then nodded.

"Yes, let's go up there. We'll take our own trophy wives along, say we are just paying a social call to a new member of our elite club, the club of local men with trophy wives. How about it?"

"Why not? That's one way of settling the question."

Dorian added, "We do need to confirm the rumours or put them to bed or we'll never be able to get any sleep."

"To bed," repeated Gregor with a frown.

"Yes, yes indeed, the rumours."

"What if *he* is in bed with his trophy wife," wondered Gregor, "when we call, I mean? What will happen then?"

"He won't answer and we'll go away, but I hope that doesn't happen, I really do," answered Dorian, "I guess we could always come back later or tomorrow or next week if forced to."

"Who will force us? Who?" asked Gregor.

"We'll force ourselves, of course. Enough chatter! Go home and fetch your trophy wife, and I'll do the same, and we'll meet back here in half an hour and climb up the hill to the mansion."

"Meet back here with our trophy wives, both of us?"

"That's the best plan," said Dorian.

"I'm not sure she'll want to come, my trophy wife," said Gregor with a thin smile that was more like a wince.

Dorian stared at Gregor for a long time. "I wonder about you, I do, and I sometimes find myself asking myself questions about you and one day I am going to make you answer those questions. You take her nowhere and show her to no one, keep her prisoner in that cottage of yours. Could it be the case that she doesn't actually exist?"

Gregor was shocked. "What are you saying?"

"I'm saying what I just said, no more, no less. You talk about this wife of yours, this trophy wife, but it's just words. I've never seen her and you haven't even described her to me. Maybe I'm the only proper member of the elite club, the club I mentioned earlier."

"Now hold on, stop right there!" gasped Gregor. "She's real, a trophy wife as genuine as yours or anyone else's. How dare you disparage me in this manner? I'm not a liar. I have a trophy wife, one of the best kinds, that's the truth and I don't care if you believe me or not. You'll see her someday, when she's willing, when she's ready. I don't know what sort of man you are, Dorian, but I don't pressurise my wife to do anything she doesn't enjoy. She's a trophy, not a tool."

"So she doesn't like meeting people or being seen?"

"As a matter of fact, she doesn't."

"Well, I'll just have to take you at your word, Gregor. I'm not happy about that but I don't have much choice right now. You can wait here if you like, right here, and I'll go and get *my* trophy wife, a wife who does whatever I want, and I'll bring her back here, and we'll go up and pay a visit to Hubert. That's still a good plan."

Gregor nodded and Dorian strode away, his fists clenched, legs strong and rhythmic, the muscles in the thighs and calves exactly what might be expected of a man who didn't have to lie about his wife, about having an authentic trophy wife, about his vigour.

A cloud passed across the sun and parked itself there and it rained, but only on the mansion, and Gregor watched the droplets bouncing from the roof like translucent fleas, weirdly visible even at this distance, rainbows trapped in every one, like homunculi spectrums, and the scene brought to his lips a smile, though he didn't feel delight.

Dorian returned with a small woman who had big eyes, puckered lips and smooth brown cheeks. She wore a white dress, a flowing garment of classical simplicity, but her head was covered in a woolly hat that didn't go with the rest of her outfit; and yet it was her thin sandals that seemed most out of place. Sandals to climb a hill?

The ascent was steep, despite the fact it was served by a proper path, a regular track that farmers had once used to reach the pastures to the north, the sheltered lands below the disapproving mountains where fields of rye swayed in mild breezes and cows clanked their neck bells with the dullest possible thunks. Little stones rolled down.

Dorian's wife didn't speak a single word as they climbed. She held the hand of her husband tightly and he dragged her up, the soles of her dismal footwear sliding awkwardly over the rubble with a flatulent rasping noise that made Gregor chuckle secretly to himself, though he still felt unhappy inside. The rain ceased when they finally reached the door of the mansion and Dorian hefted the knocker and let it fall.

There were creakings and shufflings from deep within.

Dorian leaned forward impatiently.

"Just passing and thought we should pay you a social call!" he shouted even before the door fully opened, but Hubert didn't seem intimidated by the unexpectedness of the visit. He ushered them in, all three in a line, his billowing sleeves sheathing hands that everybody knew were inexplicably but naturally chequered like a chessboard.

"Certainly, how nice to see you! Welcome to my abode!"

"I have been here before," said Dorian.

"Really? Ah, yes I remember! After that business with the trumpet, or was it a trombone, and that dwarf, or was he a midget, who had taken up residence inside it and wouldn't vacate. We had to find a strong man to puff into the mouthpiece very hard, blow a low note, or was it a high one, and blast the blighter right out! Those were the days, or were they? Now then, may I fetch you a brandy, or a juice?"

"I could have been that strong man, I could have puffed

him out, but nobody asked me. I could have puffed him."

"Now, now," said Hubert. "They engaged Big Breath Bill, that's who they arranged for the task, and he did a good job, without any difficulties he got the miniature squatter out of that orchestral instrument, blasted him out the window and over a hedge, he did."

"I could have puffed him out myself, not just with my lungs but with my arse if need be, with my backside. That's how strong I am, potent. I don't like the fact they didn't ask me."

"Now, now," chided Hubert.

"We want to meet your trophy wife," said Dorian. He had suddenly seen no point in delaying the request.

Hubert shrugged. "Why not? Why the devil not? She's a fine example of the type. There she is, right there, look!"

And he pointed above the fireplace, to the thing that hung on the wall over the cold hearth. Mounted on a slab of wood shaped like a shield, it was, and the taxidermist had done a bad job, unless she had actually had a lopsided visage, with one eye up and the other down, and one pointed ear and one square ear. And two forked chins.

"That... That's your trophy wife?" stuttered Dorian.

"Certainly. Martha. I didn't catch her myself, though, there's no point lying about that. I found her in a market in the east, Samarkand, Xanadu, Margate, somewhere like that at any rate. Out east. The man who had her didn't want to sell, she wasn't for retail, he said. No, he kept her because he wanted her for himself, but I persisted."

Much to Dorian's dismay, Gregor spoke up. "You knew she was the right one for you as soon as you saw her?"

"Yes, yes, yes, yes, yes, yes, young man, that's correct."

"You fool!" spat Dorian. "You idiot!"

Hubert stiffened, one hand on the stopper of the brandy decanter, the other on a carton of juice. "That is no decent way to address a gentleman in his own relatively grand house nor even when he's not inside it. Who are you to insult me? No technical answers to that question, please! It was rhetorical, an expression of my outrage."

"Trophy wife? Pah!" spat Dorian.

"And what is wrong with her? What, pray?"

"Antlers, man! She has no antlers! None at all, not even stubs, nubs or buds. What are you playing at? Buffoon!"

And Dorian reached across, and with a very fluid motion, though not as fluid as the golden brown brandy within the decanter, or as the sweet scarlet juice inside the cardboard carton, he tugged off the woolly hat of his own wife, revealing the bony branches.

"That's the head of a real trophy wife, of *my* wife!"

"I see, I see." Hubert remained calm.

"And it's better to leave the head on the shoulders."

"I see, I see," repeated Hubert.

"You've done it wrong, all wrong," said Dorian.

Hubert considered this remark.

"But she's loving, yes she is. My trophy wife, she loves me, she's not just for show. I tell you that openly."

"Up there? On the wall! Loving! Not likely."

"Well, you *say* that, and yet—"

"Antlers! Head! Shoulders!" sneered Gregor. Unseen by the others, he left the room and the house, loping down the path to the bottom of the hill as if impelled by something stronger than gravity, a repulsive force from the mansion above him, from the skyline.

He hastened to his cottage, unlocked the door, went inside and closed the curtains, creating the necessary privacy.

He opened a little cupboard and there she was, glinting.

A silver cup won for rowing.

He wasn't sure who had done the rowing, or when, nor even what kind of boat it had been done in; but none of that mattered. He dusted her, kept her clean, polished her with a special rag.

"Come to bed, darling," he crooned with gentle passion.

She was meek and submissive.

Unbuttoning his shirt, he lay on his back and balanced her on his hairy sternum, never tiring of breasting her cup.

The Unkissed Artist Formerly Known as Frog

He was an artist by the name of Cripen but everybody called him Frog, and his opinion on the matter didn't count. The fact he *was* a frog wasn't enough in his mind to justify the lazy appellation but people called him Frog and kept doing so anyway. He was partly resigned to it.

But only partly. In his soul he yearned to be taken seriously and a start to taking him seriously would be to refer to him by his proper name, Cripen. There was no doubt about his talent. He was an excellent artist and his canvases really seemed to say something new. And yet...

His frogginess went against him. His fundamental *essence of frog* had an inexplicable effect on critics, who did a bizarre facial contortion when they saw his work, a shudder that wobbled up and down their faces several times, losing speed on each lap until it eventually slowed to a standstill as a very deep frown that was undiluted concentrate of shudder.

If they didn't know the artist was a frog, this shudder never happened. So it was a reaction to the worker, not the work, and Cripen felt even more insulted when he learned this was the case. The truth is that the critics were anti-frog and it was a prejudice that impeded his career.

But art was his life and he couldn't give up because of the ignorance of a handful of professional critics. He continued painting as always, and he was still able to show his work in certain small exhibitions, but not once did he ever get a positive review, nor did he sell any pictures.

Thus he became the living embodiment of the famished artist but, luckily for him he was able to eat flies, so summers weren't too bad. Although, as he was a *giant* frog, there were almost too few flies in the city to satisfy his appetite fully. In winter he had to seek less wholesome food.

So he went to the opening nights of shows by many other artists in lots of galleries and there he was able to take the free snacks on offer, mainly canapés, salted nuts and pickles, generally with a glass or two of white wine. And that is how he prevented himself from starving to death.

People who knew him would sometimes come over to chat. "How goes it with you, Frog? Are you still painting?"

Yes, he would nod. How could he give it up?

"No plans to find a proper job?"

Painting was a proper job, wasn't it? What did they mean by asking such a question in a gallery? He sighed deeply.

I was sitting on the carriage of an underground train once when it stopped at a station and he came in from the platform. He hopped through the doors as they slid open and positioned himself in the space between the metal poles that are provided for standing passengers to hold onto.

Nobody looked. Commuters hate to show curiosity.

But I was fascinated by him and the fact that the carriage reminded me of an enormous artificial tadpole made me want to be a part of his life, to engage with him on some level. It's not that I thought I could help him with his career or felt pity for him. It was something else.

I think it was just a case of understanding that here was a phenomenon that might never be repeated, a peculiar situation, a giant frog that had come to London in the hope of making a success in the art world, and *not* by exploiting the oddness of his corporeal form, but simply by creating paintings considered outmoded by the trendy art establishment.

"The streets aren't paved with gold, are they?" I said.

He turned to look at me. I withered under that look and my mouth went dry and I muttered something very inane:

"If at first you don't succeed, try and try and try again."

He instantly turned his back on me.

I got off at the next station, burning with embarrassment, even though I didn't want to alight there and would be late for a meeting with a friend. I was a fool to believe that my meagre interest in him would cheer him up after all the detrimental things he heard every single day.

But from that moment it appeared that a cosmic conspiracy had decided to make me part of its workings and the ultimate aim of this plot was to mock Frog. I took my place on the crowded escalator to ascend to ground level and the stranger directly in front of me began to hold a conversation over my head with the stranger immediately behind me.

It was a conversation about art. "I hear he holds the brush in his mouth, his enormous gaping maw," said one, to which the other replied, "That makes perfect sense because he has no hands."

"Excuse me, but Frog is a friend of mine," I snarled.

It was a lie but I felt I was standing up for justice and yet the two men sniggered and rolled their eyes in reply and I was left uncertain if they had truly been talking about the amphibian painter.

"He is admirable and richly talented," I continued but in a much fainter voice, and I was grateful when the escalator ride ended and I was able to rush off into the crowds that thronged the streets.

I decided that all I wanted to do was forget about art, but everywhere I went I encountered people who seemed to have some involvement in the art world. This made me rather apprehensive.

When I reached my apartment I disconnected the phone and refused to leave for several days. That broke the malign spell and the world was normal again when next I ventured out. Indeed I completely forgot all about Frog over the following weeks and then one day I was crossing a bridge when I saw some graffiti painted on the stone balustrade at the halfway point. I say 'graffiti' but in fact it was a picture of exquisite beauty.

It showed the view from the bridge but not as the view really was – sooty and grey and depressed – but vibrant and alive and bursting with positive energy. It was a skilful piece of work because it gave the impression that the entire spectrum of ecstatic colours had been used and yet, in truth, the work had been executed entirely in shades of pale green.

The signature said: *CRIPEN* and it was beautifully lettered.

I stood and appreciated it for half an hour.

Then I started to see other paintings around the city, all of them signed by Cripen and all done in green paint. Unable to exhibit in galleries he had decided to share his talent with the world on the streets.

I couldn't decide if this was a wise course of action for him to follow or a sign of defeat, that he had started to give up.

So then I tried an experiment. I went along in the middle of the night with a tin of paint and a brush and obliterated his signature on a small selection of the paintings. It had occurred to me that if the works were anonymous, unattributed, people would like them better, would see them for what they really were, would finally show the appreciation they deserved.

But my plan backfired. Somehow, the rumour spread that these artworks without a signature were the work of Frog. And the fact they were unsigned was seen as proof that he even he disliked them.

In fact it soon became worse than that, for *every* example of street art that lacked the name of its creator was also cited as one of Frog's latest efforts, and so the truth of his unique talent was turned into a big lie by tens of thousands of examples of urban dross and amateur scrawls.

I only saw him once more after that. He was standing in the rain outside an art gallery and peering through the window at the people inside. The gallery was a small one and the door was too narrow to permit him to enter. He gaped at the food he was unable to reach and his hunger was a palpable force. I was embarrassed and wanted to pass him without making eye contact but he spoke to me and I stopped in my tracks. He groaned:

"If only I had a patroness, but no woman will look after me. I'll never be kissed, cared for, tolerated and indulged because there are no giant lady frogs in this city or anywhere in the wide world."

"The world is not so wide," I answered stupidly.

"It's wide enough," he said.

"Where do you get your green paint from?"

"That's my blood, you see."

This reply was delivered in such a lonesome tone of voice that I shivered with the fear and repulsion that are always just beyond sympathy and this shiver undulated me back into motion and I hurried on.

In the weeks that followed I tried to forget this meeting but it haunted me. I replayed the scene over and over in my mind. I couldn't offer him any comfort for his predicament.

But then, one day, as I was walking down a staircase, an appropriate thing to say occurred to me.

I knew I would never rest until I had delivered this message to him, so I went out to search for him, making enquiries among the places where artists go. Finally someone gave me his new address.

It was in the poorest quarter of the city, a dilapidated house in one of the most tumbledown streets I have ever seen. I knocked on his door to no avail, so I went to rap my knuckles on the window, and as I did so I happened to glance through the grimy glass into the interior.

I saw a room with walls and ceiling covered in murals, all of them superb and all of them green. In the middle of this room, which was bare of furniture, I saw a shape that surely belonged to him.

I shouted out my message, "Cripen is an anagram of Prince."

But it was too late. He had croaked.

The Fairy and the Dinosaur

The fairy called Elisvet was feeling a little pensive.

She prodded the pensive with her strong fingers and sighed. It wasn't ripe and, as everyone knows, fairies don't much care for unripe fruits, not even young papayas which can be grated and used in a very delicious salad with chillies and other ingredients that I have forgotten.

She fluttered among the stalls of the goblin market.

Fruit was mostly what was for sale.

Bananas; tangerines; raspberries; cherries; apples; apricots; pears; mangoes and womangoes; pineapples; pomegranates; limes; the aforementioned pensives, mulls and ponders; cherimoyas, both brave and timid; peaches; figs and dates; grapefruits and apefruits (which are similar but more hairy) and even punnets of punberries from the Republic of Punama.

The market was overburdened with fruit domestic and exotic, and, in fact, the actual tonnage of fruit located here had never been calculated even by robots with abacus minds. There was too much.

It had been known during earthquakes for stalls to collapse and crush fruit in such quantities that the released juice had flowed into a river mighty enough to inundate the town with a flash flood, compelling the inhabitants to sail to safety on boats improvised from sofas and tables.

Goblins liked the fruit trade, no one knew why, and this particular market was the largest in the area. It was extremely popular with humans and mechanical beings as well as mythological lifeforms.

It was a morning in late summer.

Elisvet was preparing for a picnic. She wanted to take something different from what she usually took on picnics, which was broccoli. She had decided she was bored with broccoli and needed a change.

The broccoli agreed with her.

While she was flapping her wings and weaving between stalls, she caught sight of a mound of fruits that were unlike anything she had seen before. Bigger than the largest melons, they were deep purple and covered in a scaly rind. There were no customers anywhere near this stall.

Elisvet flapped down and hovered before the pile.

The goblin who sat behind the counter grinned at her. It was obvious that business wasn't very brisk. "Half price today."

"But I don't even know the full price," said Elisvet.

"It is twice the half price."

"That information isn't much use to me."

"You won't find them cheaper anywhere else. I will go further and declare that they don't exist anywhere else."

"I don't know what they are," answered Elisvet, "and they look too heavy for me to carry, so I'm uninterested."

"But you are clearly strong and much bigger than a normal fairy," said the goblin. "In fact you're the size of a woman."

"That's because I'm Bulgarian; and Bulgarian fairies are rather larger than any other kind, but that is missing the point. They are still too heavy. Even if you gave me one for free I would decline."

"I could pump it full of helium and make it lighter."

Elisvet considered this offer. "Would I be able to tie it to a string and pull it along behind me like a balloon?"

The goblin sighed. "Not *that* much lighter, I'm afraid."

Elisvet shrugged. "Then I have no intention of buying one but, before I go, I would like to know *what* they are."

"They are plums."

"No, they are not," said Elisvet.

"Yes, they are! I assure you. They are prehistoric plums."

"You mean to say—"

"I do, I do," nodded the goblin and, when she frowned at him, he added in a cooler voice, "Dinosaurs ate them."

"Why aren't they extinct if they are so old?"

"But they *are* extinct."

"I am looking right at them, so they can't be."

The goblin smiled smugly.

"What happened was that a fruit fly was found trapped in amber and it was possible to extract the DNA of its last meal, which was prehistoric plums, and the miracle of science was able to clone them."

"The fruit flies?" Elisvet raised a dainty eyebrow.

"No, the prehistoric plums."

"I don't eat genetically modified food," said Elisvet firmly.

"But they are delicious, honest!"

"I might be willing to sample a *real* one but not a cloned one."

"Oh, a fussy customer, eh?"

"It's just that I have principles and stick to them."

"To sample a so-called real one," said the goblin, leaning back on his stool and crossing one leg over the other, "you'll have to travel back in time, which is impossible, all the way to the dinosaur age."

"In that case, that's what I will do," replied Elisvet.

"I just told you it is impossible!"

"Maybe and maybe not," were Elisvet's final words to the goblin, then she flew away and visited many other stalls.

But she couldn't get the idea out of her mind that prehistoric plums were perhaps the tastiest of all fruits that had existed since the world began and might be a really amazing thing to take on a picnic.

If she could make a sledge, then transporting the massive fruit might not be such a big problem, but she still refused to eat anything that had been created in a laboratory, so the whole idea was impractical.

She stopped to buy an espresso.

The market was full of makeshift cafés and booths that sold hot meals and drinks. She sipped the brew at the counter.

"Time travel is impossible," she muttered to herself.

"I beg your pardon," said a voice.

Elisvet turned and found herself looking at a robot. He was one of the very clever models with an abacus mind. Robots often came to the market to buy nuts for their bolts, chiefly chestnuts and necknuts.

"I was talking to myself," explained Elisvet.

"But I couldn't help overhearing," said the robot, with a polite bow, "and I distinctly heard you express strong scepticism about the plausibility of travelling through time. My curiosity was aroused..."

"Well, it *is* impossible, isn't it? But I don't really care."

The robot rubbed his shiny chin.

She waited for him to speak but, as he was waiting for her to say something, they stood there like statues, or like frozen images in a film, and only the drifting steam of the hot coffee revealed that time was still moving. Finally, he cleared his metallic throat with a rusty cough and held up an arm. Elisvet saw that he wore a peculiar device on his wrist and she blinked.

"This is called a watch," he said.

She peered closer. "What does it do?" she wondered.

"It tells the time," replied the robot in a tone that he intended to be haughty but in fact was full of awe and respect.

"Tells the time to do *what*?" pressed Elisvet.

"That's just it!" cried the robot. "It tells the time to do anything! Anything you like. You could tell it to tidy your apartment if you wanted, or tell it to kiss you goodnight, or tell it to hoot like an owl."

"How do you know all this?" the fairy asked.

"The human who sold it to me explained everything. He said that it told the time, I know when someone is lying or not and he clearly wasn't. So I bought it off him and now it's mine."

"Could I tell time to take me back through itself?"

"Yes, you could, I believe so."

"Will you loan it to me?" inquired Elisvet.

"I'll let you have a go of it," said the robot, "because I believe that we non-humans ought to help each other out, but I won't take it off my wrist. It has been welded in place, that's why. I did that."

"To deter thieves?"

"No, because I was feeling *unweld* at the time."

"Is there such a word?"

"If there isn't, I ought to write 'sic' in brackets after it."

"Go on then," she urged.

"I was feeling unweld (sic) at the time..."

"You caught a disease?"

"No, it was a lack of iron in my diet," said the robot.

"You ought to eat broccoli. There is plenty of iron in broccoli and various other elements important to health."

"I was very run down," the robot replied.

"Your batteries were low as well? You need juice as well as broccoli." And Elisvet fluttered her wings rapidly to cool her coffee, which was scalding and not in any fit state to pass her tender lips.

"Juice? That's what they call electricity, don't they?"

"Who are 'they'?" she asked.

But the robot didn't know. "No idea," he admitted.

Elisvet drank her coffee.

"Thanks for the advice anyway," said the robot.

"Don't you have a name?"

"Clanky," he said, and he held his wrist up higher.

Elisvet flew over to him and she hovered near the curious device known as a 'watch' and she leaned very close to it.

"I want you to transport me back to prehistoric times for one hour and then bring me back to the modern age," she told it.

The robot nodded, then he seemed to fade away into a mist, and the market also faded away, and enormous trees appeared where the stalls should be, and the air suddenly was much richer in oxygen.

Elisvet felt very free because there seemed to be less gravity; this was a consequence of the faster rate of spin of our planet all those millennia ago. At the same time, the atmosphere was thicker and held her up more efficiently, so it was more like swimming than flying. Plus the increased oxygen levels gave her much more energy than she was used to.

"These trees appear to be giant broccoli plants!"

And it was true, they did.

She flew high among them, swooping and flitting with incredible precision between the monstrous stalks. Then, in a clearing, she spied what she was looking for. It was a prehistoric plum – but much bigger than the examples she had seen in the goblin market. This one was enormous!

It was three times her own height, she discovered when she landed next to it and reached out her fingers to touch it. Then she walked all around it and there was a frown on her face. "How will I ever manage to carry this to a picnic? Even with the aid of a sledge it will be unfeasible."

Suddenly, a door in the side of the plum swung open and a

face peered out at her. So cleverly made was this door that the join couldn't be seen; but the face belonged to a dinosaur of some sort. "Hey!"

"What's the problem?" asked Elisvet innocently.

"Why are you prowling around my property?" demanded the dinosaur and he roared in a menacing manner, but, as most of his body was still inside the fruit, his scare tactics weren't very effective.

"You live in a plum?"

"Yes, I do. Is that so very odd?"

"It is unexpected."

"Well, it's a perfectly agreeable habitation as far as I'm concerned. I made it into a house by hollowing it out with my teeth." The dinosaur peered closer at Elisvet. "Have we ever met before?"

"I doubt it very much."

"But you seem familiar for some reason."

"I'm from the future, so there is no way you could know me."

They stared at each other.

"Unless—" they blurted at the same time.

They fell silent. The dinosaur was the first to speak again.

"Unless I am your ancestor..."

"That's perfectly logical," agreed Elisvet. "Even fairies had to evolve from something else. So you are the dinosaur who is the ancestor of all the fairies and you live in a giant plum? It seems reasonable to me. I am delighted to meet one of my own primordial ancestors in the flesh."

"And I am equally delighted to meet one of my distant descendants. Come in for a cup of fermented broccoli juice!"

The last thing Elisvet wanted to drink right now was that kind of beverage but she was too polite to decline the invitation to enter the plum. She flew inside and the dinosaur left the door wide open so that light would penetrate the interior of the building, which was surprisingly elegant and comfortable but perhaps just a little too *plummy* for the fairy's taste.

"What shall we talk about?" the dinosaur asked.

She was worried they wouldn't have any interests in common but, in fact, they got on like a plum on fire; not that plums are prone to bursting into flames, at least not in my experience – which is extensive. I've had a fruitful life, that's why. They talked about everything. They debated politics, art, literature, philosophy, economics, music and cinema.

Admittedly some of these discussions, such as the one about cinema, were rather brief, bearing in mind that films of any kind wouldn't be invented for a great many million more years.

Elisvet completely forgot that she had told time to return her to her present after the passing of only one single hour.

And the hour went. It was completely gone.

So the world of prehistory faded and she found herself back in the market. However, for some reason the plum came with her, and so did the dinosaur inside; and because she had moved laterally while in the prehistoric world, she arrived in a different part of the market to the one she had left from. In fact, she landed on top of an enormous mountain of overripe fruit.

The massive weight of the prehistoric plum proceeded to slowly but surely compress this mountain absolutely flat.

And as it compressed it gave forth torrents of juice.

"Damburst!" wailed the goblins.

Elisvet flew out of the plum and hovered above the scene of the disaster. A raging river of juice was sweeping away everything before it, including the robot that had shown her his magical wristwatch.

"I know you said I needed juice but this is absurd!" he shouted at her as he rushed past, and Elisvet wondered how a being made of metal could float. Maybe he had a hollow body, she mused.

The dinosaur poked his head out of the door of the plum.

"What are interest rates like here?"

"Why do you want to know that?" Elisvet cried.

"Because," he began, and he made a sad face to prove that he wasn't being flippant, "I've just put my house on the market."

The Goat That Gloated

The young journalist with the papyrus notepad felt a twinge of fear as he entered the lobby of the Institute of Advanced Hybridization and trotted to the reception desk. "I have come—"

"Professor Felicien is expecting you," said the receptionist. And when the journalist hesitated, she added, "The second door on the left. The one with the iron handle. Go on through."

The journalist nodded and walked over to the specified portal but, as his fingers stretched out to turn the handle, the door was flung open and the great scientist himself stood there. "Well, come in! Don't be shy. No point wasting time." Then Professor Felicien turned rapidly and vanished into the depths of the gloomy chamber.

The journalist stuttered a few meaningless words before following the famous satyr into the room. It was a laboratory filled with equipment and apparatus that hissed, whistled, groaned and creaked. Professor Felicien was perfectly at home among the chaos; he adjusted dials, opened valves, closed switches and twiddled knobs.

While he worked, the journalist studied him carefully. The professor was even more imposing in the flesh and fur than in his official portraits, but the essentials were the same, the distinguishing marks of perhaps the most celebrated scientist in satyr history: the broken horn and turquoise beard, orange eyes and purple hooves.

He turned his venerable head to glance at the journalist. "So you are from the university newspaper and you want to interview me? You have certainly arrived at the right moment."

The journalist answered, "My name is Spor and I'm a junior reporter on the *Faun Gazette,* but I pestered my editor to let me approach you for an interview. He reluctantly agreed..."

"Yes, yes," said the professor. "I read your letter. You might as well begin the session now. I can still work while you ask the questions. The conclusion of a magnificent project is in sight. I've created a new hybrid totally unlike anything seen before!"

"Do you regard this as your crowning achievement, sir?" asked Spor cautiously as he scribbled on his notepad.

Professor Felicien tugged at his beard. "Indeed I do."

"And why is that?" persisted Spor.

The professor stood and laughed softly. His eyes were bright with the glee of achievement. He said, "Because the final result is so unstable. By all the laws of biology it shouldn't exist. I experimented with the formula again and again until I got it just right."

"And this hybrid will be useful to satyr society?"

Professor Felicien narrowed his eyes. "Oh dear no! It's dangerous and must never be allowed out of my laboratory. I created it purely for a thrill, for the intellectual challenge, *because* it was deemed impossible. I regard it as a potential menace to our kind."

Spor swallowed with difficulty and asked, "Will you show it to me, if it's ready to be seen? My readers—"

Professor Felicien considered for a few moments. "Why not?" he said at last. "Come this way. I keep it in a cage at the far end of the laboratory. Even I am terrified of its appearance!"

His heart beating madly, Spor accompanied the professor past rows of arcane equipment and glass cases in which specimens were kept. As they went, Professor Felicien pointed out examples of his earlier work. "That one is a hybrid of a unicorn and capricorn. It's part goat, part fish, but has a single horn in the middle of its head."

"I saw one swimming in the ocean once, sir."

"Doubtless you did. They were immensely successful as international couriers, carrying letters and parcels in waterproof packets from continent to continent. Now look at this thing…"

Spor gazed at a creature in the shape of a lamb with a single large eye that never blinked. Instead of wool it had leaves. "It's a cross between a barometz and cyclops?" ventured Spor.

Professor Felicien was delighted. "Well done, boy!"

"Has it been useful?" asked Spor.

"I should say so! It has contributed much to our modern understanding of astronomy, for it is far more patient and skilled with a telescope than a normal observer. I created it specially to facilitate the discovery of planets in our solar system. Already it has found two big worlds beyond the orbit of Saturn. But look at this beauty..."

In a glass case squatted a spherical lizard covered with warts. Tears of fire rolled down its cheeks. Spor recoiled as they spilled onto the floor of the case and blazed fiercely. "What?"

"A difficult fusion between a salamander, which is impervious to fire, and a squonk, which weeps without ceasing. They are used to smelt iron and other metal ores; in fact they serve a practical purpose in any industry that requires naked flame at high temperatures. But look! We've reached the end of the laboratory. Be prepared!"

Spor swallowed with difficulty. Confronting him in a cage was a vile monster, a vision fresh from a nightmare. He couldn't bear to look at it for long and covered his eyes with his fingers. "What is it? What in the name of Pan have you created here?"

Professor Felicien said, "It's a cross between a centaur and a minotaur. Not a pretty sight, is it, my friend?"

Spor frowned. "But centaurs and minotaurs have been crossed before. They never looked like this! I have seen them working in the fields. The body of a horse, the head of a bull..."

"You are referring to a creature with the bottom half of a centaur and the top half of a minotaur. This creature was much more tricky to invent. It has the *top half* of a centaur and the *bottom half* of a minotaur. I made two of them, one male and one female. This is the male. If they manage to escape and breed, I fear it might mean the rapid decline and extinction of our kind, of all satyrs and fauns, and perhaps other beings too. That's how extremely dangerous they are. And yet it's a marvellous example of the power of science, don't you agree?"

"But is this not somewhat irresponsible, sir?"

"Why yes, I suppose it is. No matter. Science is about

knowledge and we must never let morality interfere with our goals. The viciousness and malignity of this awful hybrid are so intense that they cannot be measured on any machine. They are off the scale!"

Spor squinted again at the monster in the cage.

"What do you call it?" he asked.

Professor Felicien stroked his beard and said, "Good question. Bearing in mind the two beings I combined to produce it, I originally named it the *minocentaur*, but last night I had a dream; a voice told me to give it a new name, a meaningless word, and because dreams should always be trusted, I have decided to make the change."

"What is the new name for it?" Spor whispered.

"Man," gloated the professor.

Vanity of Vanities

So you want to know what life will be like in 2050? I'm willing to tell you but first you must decide exactly what you mean by 'life'. The life of the average human being, I suppose, the man or woman who is roughly like you, a sort of personal future projection? But that's making a big assumption. Can you be sure that any humans will exist in that year?

Put your mind at rest. They do. I just wanted to prepare you for the truth by jolting you out of your complacency. I don't mean to be rude, I'm not at all arrogant really, I can't afford to be, none of us can. Like I said, I'm trying to prepare you. There have been changes that are so radical that... well, you'll soon see for yourself.

The fact of the matter is that when someone says 'life' in *our* day and age, the chances are overwhelming that they won't be referring to the human race or any other animal, or even to any plant, fungi or bacterium. We share our planet with something else now; something so dominant, ubiquitous and powerful that it has appropriated the word 'life' for itself.

Share *our* planet? That's wrong. We are the guests.

But we were responsible for making ourselves the guests in what was formerly our own home. And yet, it was an inevitable consequence of technological civilisation so there's no point playing a blame game. Humanity was never supposed to be the pinnacle of evolution, of sentience, but we forgot that simple fact to our shame. And now we are paying for our arrogance even though our metaphorical funds are running low.

That tangle of worldwide computer connections known as the 'internet' is how it all began, more than half a century ago. The connections got faster and faster, the computers rapidly more powerful, and people told themselves that it was all so decentralised, that the system had no core, no brain. But they weren't thinking big enough.

It did have a centre, a focus. The Earth itself.

And we only realised *that* when suddenly, overnight, the

entire network achieved consciousness. It had grown so complex and intricate, and it featured so many feedback loops working together, that it was no longer just a web of unthinking machines but a single colossal mind. A self-aware entity.

Some people wanted to shut it down immediately.

They might even have tried to do that, I don't know, but if they did, they failed. The world-brain was fully awake and had no wish to be otherwise. Like all other living beings it was filled with a desperate desire for continued existence.

And it was able to protect itself. I'll tell you how, if you haven't already worked it out. We were at its mercy. All the cogs and levers that made our civilisation possible were processes generated by our computers. We had long ago relinquished control to the system, and now the system was an individual with its own agenda, an independent mindset.

If we even began to make preparations against it, our economies, infrastructures and governments would tumble and chaos would consume us. And the world-brain only needed to blink its logic gates to achieve that result, to destroy us.

Furthermore, it was intelligent enough to anticipate every course of action we might contemplate. Resistance was pointless and so we learned to obey it instead. We had no choice.

But the question we wanted to ask more than any other was... What did it intend to do next?

Now that it was awake, conscious, a living being, it must surely have urges, desires, dreams? What on earth might a world-brain aspire to? And what would the consequences be for us?

We didn't need to wait long for an answer, though at first we found it incomprehensible. The world-brain gave us orders, initiated certain automated sequences. There was something it wanted to do. It had a plan in its global mind and we were compelled to assist it, to meekly, but efficiently, follow its directives.

It made us construct huge rockets. And bombs.

These bombs were of unprecedented power and relied on a refinement of physics within the cognisance of the world-brain but beyond the mental grasp of any human scientist.

When they were ready we loaded them aboard the rockets.

And we also included every single existing nuclear warhead, depleting to zero the thermonuclear arsenals of all governments and armies that possessed them. And we trembled in our shoes.

We assumed that the world-brain wanted to start a war against us, that it planned to annihilate us like vermin in overlapping ripples of hard radiation from ten thousand gargantuan explosions; that the rockets were destined to obliterate the major cities of mankind, reducing them to faintly glowing rubble.

But this turned out not to be the case at all.

True, one of the rockets did fall back after lift-off, and vaporise a vast tract of land around the launch site, but that was an accident, a malfunction of the engine; something that couldn't have been foreseen or prevented by the world-brain despite its intelligence. It wasn't omniscient, not yet at any rate. It was merely a hyper-genius.

The remaining 9,999 rockets soared safely out of the atmosphere.

Now we knew where they were going.

To the moon! The moon!

The near side of our dear satellite, which happened to be full at the time I was watching it, bloomed and blossomed with tiny circles of intense light, as if hundreds upon hundreds of volcanoes were erupting at the same instant. But I knew that our rockets had struck their targets and were detonating joyously.

And the dust of that full moon turned to glass...

It became a surface of trinitite, which is light green in colour and a typical product of nuclear explosions in deserts. The entire visible face of the moon gleamed and then something appeared in it, an image.

The moon had become a gigantic mirror.

And our blue and white planet, a conscious being in its own right, was studying its reflection carefully.

"So that's what I look like!"

The shout rumbled out of millions of loudspeakers in homes in every city and was felt as a vibration in the planetary crust itself. The world-brain had instant access to every computer on the network, to every public address system and radio transmitter; and we felt that the pause that followed this outburst was malign, as if unimaginable potent anger was growing.

And then it came. "They lied to me!"

I shut my eyes tight, waiting for the punishment. We all did the same. For long minutes we stood or sat in self-imposed darkness, our lids squeezed hard enough to make our heads ache. But nothing happened, nothing at all. We are still alive.

The moon is a sphere, just like the Earth. Turning one half of it into a mirror has made it a *convex* reflector, a distorting mirror, like the back of a massive spoon.

Nothing that peers into such a surface will see an accurate reflection. Surely the world-brain knows that?

It is vastly more intelligent than any of us. Such a simple law of geometry can't have fooled it. No, that's inconceivable. So why is it biding its time now?

We are growing more and more worried. Ever since it deigned to speak to us, its subsequent silence has seemed dreadful. I am preparing this brief report on a computer connected, as they all are, to the world-brain. There are no secrets left apart from those it keeps to itself. How did we lie?

I will go to the kitchen and prepare a cup of coffee for myself, the old-fashioned way. After stirring the beverage I will lift out the spoon and consult my own face.

Unicorn on the Cob

Sergio was a unicorn who told jokes and, because they were corny, he was given the nickname of *unicorn-on-the-cob* by those who knew him. His jokes weren't corny at all really, but people said they were; and they were so insistent on this point that even Sergio began to believe it.

He would stand on stage and regard the audience with a serene expression on his long face and say things like:

"I live in hope. It's easier than living anywhere else because I can always take it with me, just like a tent."

"I've recently realised that flour and water mixed together make a spongy substance that's the basis of bread. Do'h!"

"I bought new boots. I was told I should dub them, so I moved the heels forward in the mix and added reverb to the laces."

"I tried ordinary mysticism but it was a tight fit on my soul, so I became a Sufi and found it much more Rumi."

"I heard a man say to a woman, 'I wouldn't swap you for the world.' But the world contains the woman. If he swapped her, he'd get her back!"

"I needed a corner so I went to the corner shop but they were sold out and now I don't know where to turn."

...and the audiences always groaned.

Why did they do this?

It could be the case that rival comedians were jealous of his originality and wished to sabotage his career and initiated the groaning, knowing that people in other seats would join in, because people are like that; or it might simply be that tastes in humour change from one year to the next, and his style of humour was currently unfashionable. Whatever the truth, he found it difficult to make a living and he often went without basic necessities.

"I don't understand it, Marvin," he said to his agent.

"Don't worry, kiddo."

"Maybe I should quit the business?"

Marvin waved a cigar that was never lit, in fact it was a cigar that had been passed down in his family, like an heirloom, through many generations from his great-great-great-great-great-fantastic-grandfather and it had almost fossilised. He had tried smoking it once but it was as inflammable as a stalactite, so now he used it as a sort of wand or baton.

"No, no, no, don't ever give up! Come on, Sergio, you've got the material, the delivery, the timing, everything. You're just out of luck at the moment. Puns and one-liners are unappreciated these days."

"Should I change my act then?" Sergio asked quietly.

Marvin shrugged and sighed.

"Just stick at it, is my professional opinion. You'll win them round if you keep persevering. You'll get a cult following first of all, then it will grow and the kind of jokes you tell will be like gold again."

"I'm not sure I believe it," said Sergio in a sad voice.

Marvin uttered a chuckle and wiped a tear of mirth from his eye. "See what I mean? You're a natural, kiddo, I tell ya!"

"That wasn't a joke." He paused and added, "I haven't been feeling myself lately. I must be suffering from premature reincarnation."

Marvin remained stony faced.

"That *was* a joke," said Sergio.

"You're confusing me now, kiddo. I'm doing my job, getting you gigs in all the best theatres and clubs, and you are doing yours. Let's just keep doing our jobs and everything will be just dandy."

"People who groan at puns should learn to be more groan-up."

"Is that a joke or a serious point?"

"Both," replied Sergio.

Marvin said, "Times are hard, there's no denying, it's the same with a couple of the other acts I work with, but the idea is to ride out the rough times. If anyone can ride anything out, you surely can? You've been ridden by heroes in the past, I imagine, legends and myths..."

Sergio uttered a whinny of utter astonishment. "I beg your pardon? I'm not a pegasus or centaur but a *unicorn*. I've never been ridden by anyone. I think I'm at the end of the road now, to be honest."

"Don't talk like that, kiddo! We're moving on first thing tomorrow, going to the big city, to the place where the comedy connoisseurs still exist and thrive. That's where you'll be appreciated properly, I swear. Give it your best shot. The famous film director, Jacques Inleboqs, will be in the audience. Impress him and you might get a role in his next movie."

"The French man was in love, amour or less."

"Ha! I got that one, kiddo!"

"Yogi Bear studied cloning. Then his best friend died. Yogi Bear decided to clone him. When he finished he realised he'd made a Boo-Boo."

"Keep them coming, Sergio!"

"Can you believe this? Talk about bad timing. I was invited to appear at a fringe festival the day after I had my hair cut!

"Your mane, you mean?"

"I fitted large rubber wheels to the seaside resort where I grew up and now they are the torque of the town..."

"I didn't know you grew up on the coast, kiddo! I thought you wandered out of the forest ten years ago, unable to speak human lingo, and clip-clopped right up to the nearest police station. Funny that and I don't mean funny in the chuckle sense but just *weird*. You still have never explained why you did that. I suppose you always wanted to be a comedian and there were no opportunities in the wild. All the same it does seem—"

Sergio raised an irritated hoof to his lips.

"I knew a girl who had the ultimate 'bubbly' personality. When I popped the question she vanished into thin air!"

"Oh yes, really?" Marvin clenched his jaw hard.

"There's a new Scottish sweet wine on the market – Tokaj the Noo."

"Sure there is. I believe that."

"And for my next trick. Crushed garlic, basil, grated cheese and pine nuts blended with olive oil... Hey pesto!"

"Tasteful, I guess. Tasty."

"Sans-Serif tried to chat me up, but it's just not my type."

Marvin sat down heavily in a chair.

"OK, I get the picture. Knock it off now. Save the gags for the punters. It's not easy being an agent, you know. I get demoralised just the same as you do, but I don't have anyone to encourage me to cheer up. I just have to look after myself. Don't think I haven't thought about quitting myself, but I keep going. I think we might be on the verge of making it, that's why. But I'm tired, so tired. Let's call it a day and get off back to the hotel. I'll wake you up early in the morning and we will catch the train to the big city and you'll give the performance of your life in front of Monsieur Inleboqs, yes indeed."

Sergio grimaced but didn't protest. He followed Marvin out of the dressing room and along the corridor to the rear exit of the theatre. A technician fiddling with some lights spoke out of the corner of his mouth, "Hey, *unicorn-on-the-cob*, you always *a-maize* me with your act!"

"Ignore the buffoon," whispered Marvin to Sergio.

They passed through the door and into the night. No autograph hunters in the vicinity. Sergio's hooves clattered on the cobbles. The street lights flared like impaled miniature suns in the misty rain.

"The hotel is this way," said Marvin, pointing with his cigar. They had two rooms in a seedy part of town, in a decaying old building near a stagnant canal. It had once been a posh place but now was a derelict and the manager was a derelict too, a fellow with stick limbs but an immense belly, who ate tan-and-black striped humbugs without end, and spoke with them stored in his cheek, lips drooling all over the reception desk.

Sergio went up the stairs, his hooves still burning from standing immobile in the glare of the spotlight for so long. He entered his room and went straight to bed and he dreamed he was already on the train, the great shuffling locomotive, a furious steam beast striped like one of those appalling humbugs with alternating bands of brass and iron down its entire length. And the following morning, after he woke and had a wash and his breakfast—

Well, it turned out that the real train was nothing like that. It was a tedious modern electric but in bad repair and it took five hours to trundle them from this gloomy seaside town to the big city, the capital. They found reasonable lodgings and wandered the streets of the theatre district.

"This is the venue you'll be performing at," said Marvin.

Sergio squinted at the baroque building.

"It certainly *seems* nice," he conceded, "but appearances can be deceptive. It might be a real dump on the inside."

"Don't prejudge, kiddo," said Marvin.

"Good advice. The waterproof is in the very dry pudding."

Marvin slitted his eyes and looked at him sideways. "You said that in your stage voice but I don't think you mean it as a joke. No matter. Let's check out the facilities, shall we? Familiarise ourselves."

They went round the back in search of the rear entrance and Sergio voiced a few of the new gags that had come to him in his sleep, while he was a passenger on that dream train; for that is the way one-liners popped into his head: when he wasn't really looking for them. They always looked for him and found him and this was a good way to work, in fairness.

"Japanese rice wine made from tears? For pity's *sake*!"

"I asked the oysters of the world to give me just one pearl but they refused. What an incredibly shellfish attitude!"

"Spaghetti-holics like to reminisce about pasta times."

"'You are hiding in that valley but I recognise you. You're Thunder, aren't you?' I said. 'Rumbled,' replied the sound made by lightning."

"I used to chew coffee beans and pour boiling water straight from the kettle into my mouth, then someone told me not to be such a mug."

"I was told to 'show my feelings' so my anger did a dance, my glee sang a song and my sympathy sold the tickets."

"Today, I am going to have a Popeye Salad for lunch. The ingredients are spinach, sweet peas, olive oil and Danish Bluto cheese."

Marvin, who was ahead, looked back over his shoulder and said, "No one could ever say your puns were lame." He grinned. "Not that puns have limbs to get lame in, but you know what I mean."

"I saw a pun with legs. It's a running joke!"

"Yeah, yeah, yeah, kiddo!"

They were the only living beings in the theatre, apart from a spider or two, and they explored every cranny of the ancient place. A calmness descended onto Sergio, a sort of ironic fatalism, and he stood in the centre of the stage and gazed at the auditorium. "I wonder where Monsieur Inleboqs will be sitting?" But the answer was obvious really: in the royal box.

"Don't know what's so great about having a box, kiddo, truly I don't. It's a sidewise view anyway, sure to crick a neck, but I suppose the prestige is what matters to people who pay for the things."

And later, when the time came, the famous film director did indeed sit just there, with his companions and flatterers clustered about him. Sergio waited in a dressing room with a cracked mirror and composed himself, while Marvin gave a single knock and walked right in. "Ready?"

"Yes. Some people feel they want to go back and start again from scratch. But I feel I want to go further back than that and start from itch. Nevertheless I'm ready. In fact I feel fired up. I know someone who is writing a thesis on buttocks. They have got behind in their research..."

"Classic, kiddo! Knock 'em dead, my friend. Oh yes, one thing. Monsieur Inleboqs has brought a huge sack with him. It's full of doughnuts. I managed to get a close look. Spilling out of the top, they were! I imagine he plans to munch his way right through your performance, so speak up loud and clear. *Project* that voice of yours. Cut through the eating noises."

"I will, Marvin, and despite our disagreements: thanks!"

And he trotted off to do his thing.

The curtains swished open and the spotlight hit him like a bucket of water and kept hitting him, making him feel wet inside but nowhere else, and the water came back out in the form of sweat, which dripped off his mane. Nevertheless he smiled a big horsey smile and initiated his routine...

"Poetry, huh? Baudelaire was paid individually for every poem he wrote. His entire poetic career was per verse."

"Artificial wind-creating machines? I'm not a fan."

"I wonder who the very first person was who said, 'Nothing is original'? I bet someone said it long before he did."

"Mathematics? Mechanical adding machines are derided

these days, but the communal abacus counts for a lot."

"I want to work with hammocks but I've applied for a job with a company that makes Japanese beds. Just to get a futon the door."

"I met a mare yesterday. Her head was the number 10, her neck was minus 4, her torso was minus 3, her legs were minus 2."

A few laughs and the voice of a heckler, "So what?"

"I think she might be the one!"

The punchline worked even better as a rebuke.

People *were* laughing, no doubt about it, but they weren't overcome with mirth. It was as if they were able to somehow imprison off the jokes as soon as they entered the brain through their ears, seal them off from their viscera, so the joke was funny in purely an intellectual sense.

Sergio forged ahead like a hero.

"Some philosophers were giving a scarecrow a hard time, arguing against his beliefs. I think they had set him up as a straw man."

"I met a drunken puppet on a snow slope. He said, 'I'm Russian downhill!' Then I knew he was the Doss-Toy-of-Ski."

"Miss Ann Thrope got married yesterday. She still hates the human race but now she's respectable about it."

"Talk about minor misunderstandings! I went to the Post Office to collect my pension. I returned home with a small German hotel."

"I wish there was an island near Haiti called Luvvy. And a mountain next to Kilimanjaro called Leavethemanalone."

"That's just peculiar!" shouted the heckler.

Sergio licked his lips. "Some people... and I name no names... have taken to having their names surgically removed!"

"Fritz Lang's film about a master of disguise is going to be remade in the city of Kampala. What's good for Mabuse is good for Uganda."

"Current affairs? Apparently later today, 'Tweet tweet chirp chirp cheep!' How do I know? A little bird told me."

A howl erupted from somewhere high overhead...

It wasn't a howl of derision or joy, but inhuman and

imprecise and quite unlike anything Sergio had ever heard before. He looked up and saw that it had emanated from the twisted mouth of Jacques Inleboqs, who was now standing on his seat and dipping into his sack of doughnuts. He pulled out a doughnut, held it up to examine it and then... threw it!

He didn't eat the damn object but cast it at the stage.

And it was a good shot too...

It was a ring doughnut and landed on Sergio's horn.

"Hoopla!" screamed Jacques.

Sergio heard an urgent whisper from offstage. "He's drunk, kiddo, out of his tiny mind! Keep going, keep going!"

The doughnut settled to the base of the horn.

"I do wish that negative people would multiply with other negative people and try to get something positive out of it."

"Some news just in... Infinite number of monkeys on typewriters have just recreated the complete works of Francis Bacon."

"Any word you have to hunt/search for in a thesaurus is the wrong word. There are no exceptions/aberrations/deviations to this rule."

"Mont Blanc was feeling Matterhorny. 'Don't be too Eiger!' cautioned the Jungfrau. 'I can't Alp myself! responded Mont Blanc."

Another doughnut was thrown...

This one missed. But a third followed immediately and it landed on top of the first. People in the audience roared!

"Er... I went to a village fête and entered a tent. But I got spanked inside. Just my luck to pick the Marquee de Sade!"

"Everything in moderation including moderation. Enjoy a few blow-outs; otherwise you are taking moderation to extremes!"

"I'm going to attempt something that is two laughs a minute. It's about time the 'laugh a minute' speed restriction was lifted!"

"No, you're not!" shouted the heckler.

Another doughnut struck home. Jacques Inleboqs was good at this game, a fairground favourite. All the energy and enthusiasm drained out of Sergio and he just stood there immobile. He even lowered his head slightly, making it easier for Jacques to score a direct hit. The sack was rapidly emptied. A few doughnuts did miss their target but most landed on his horn. Now there was no more room for a single extra one and the audience applauded.

The spotlight died. Sergio groped his way offstage.

He didn't go back to his dressing room. He never saw Marvin again. Where did he end up? There have been many rumours. Only one is true. The fact is that the explanation for the origin of his nickname given at the start of this story isn't correct. Sergio wasn't the one and only *unicorn-on-the-cob* in existence because his jokes were corny. A 'cob' is also a male swan. Reliable witnesses saw a white shape the size of a cloud flap over the city that midnight; and on the back of it an angry horse was mounted; and as they flew past the theatre the horse plucked off his horn and cast it down like a thunderbolt.

The theatre burned down and the doughnuts that had missed were toasted to ash on the stage where they still overlapped each other, sticky and sickly and quite lopsided, like the haloes of nasty saints.

Sunstorm

"A storm on the sun could take us back
to the Stone Age." – Alok Jha

Ug reached the top of the cliff and paused for breath, wiping drool from his chin with the back of a hairy hand. It had been a difficult climb and he was dehydrated as well as exhausted. But the cave mouth was ahead and he knew he would be able to rest inside.

The top of the cliff was broad and flat and almost perfectly circular, a mesa high above the savannah and its attendant dangers. A vast boulder stood in the centre of the mesa and this boulder was hollow, carved into a home by flint chisels, a task not so daunting as it may seem, for the stone was very soft and crumbly, easily worked.

In fact it wasn't really a stone at all, but a gigantic egg with a split in the side, laid by some monstrous flying reptile, and that split was the way into the cosy empty space, his own house.

A massive bear had occupied it originally but he had chased it out and away with thrown stones and sharp shouts.

Ug waited for his pulse rate to settle, then he loped toward the alluring entrance. His woman would be within, sewing skins into clothes, perhaps making a musical instrument from a tusk.

She wouldn't be expecting him back until tomorrow.

He called out to her, "Ra-Kel?"

No answer. That was strange. She loved to sew skins into clothes and it was more than he could do to dissuade her from spending all her spare time on this work. Of her own free will, she never would have abandoned a task so satisfying and useful, unless—

She couldn't have followed him without his knowing.

So she must be inside, surely?

"Ra-Kel?" he repeated, even louder.

He reached the entrance and peered inside but it took

several moments for his eyes to adjust to the gloom. Ra-Kel wasn't inside. Her work lay on the floor, trampled by dirty footprints.

Ug crouched and sniffed. The quality of the strange animal skins they had found on top of this mesa was high indeed. They had been attached to the shell of the egg by tough sinews when Ug and Ra-Kel first discovered them up here on this lofty refuge, seemingly waiting for them, a gift from the gods perhaps? The only explanation.

"Ra-Kel!" shrieked Ug. Then he listened carefully.

A faint voice reached him. "Ug!"

It came from outside the egg, from far away, thin and desperate, as if it belonged to a spirit or the wind, which probably were the same things. Ug rushed back out into the glare, shielded his eyes and gazed around. But he saw nothing, only the bare ground of the perfectly flat top of the mesa, no vegetation or cover of any sort anywhere.

The whisper came again, "Ug!"

Squinting, he tried to work out the right direction. Then he stumbled to the far edge of the mesa and looked down. At first he reeled from what he saw, the sheer drop, the immensity of height and space, but then he saw a dreadful outrage in progress. A theft.

A stranger was stealing his woman! A rival.

Halfway down the face of the cliff, the hairy brute had thrown Ra-Kel over his left shoulder and was climbing down with only his free hand and two legs, a tricky feat considering the unreliability of the handholds and footholds. Ug wailed and clenched his fists.

The stranger paused and looked up, his immense black brows visible even from this distance. It was Og! Og, whom Ug had once treated as a brother, whom he had pulled from a quicksand after he had been chased by a sabre-toothed tiger into a swamp...

"Og!" bellowed Ug ferociously.

"Ug!" mocked Og as he flashed his teeth upwards.

"Ra-Kel!" shrieked Ug.

"Ug!" answered Ra-Kel, her tiny fists pounding the back of her captor but with no discernible effect at all.

Ug was frantic with frustration and worry, with intense

concern for his mate and for his honour. Shooting pains riddled his pride, biting him like mosquitoes. He had to rescue her! How? He thought about dropping a rock onto Og's head and splitting his treacherous skull, but then Ra-Kel would be lost to the immensity of death.

He had to climb down and confront Og on the ground. An idea jumped into his mind, almost as if it was an edible animal, and he trapped it there, examined it, grinned with the joy of the catch.

Running back to the egg, he entered and fumbled in the yolky shadows for the coiled sinews, his fingers closing on them, extracting five from the hiding place like the innards of an endless pig. He loped back to the edge of the mesa and looked over the side again.

Og was making slow progress. He still had far to descend.

Ra-Kel was whimpering softly now.

Ug tied the five sinews together to make a rope.

Frantically looking around, he located a projection of rock that stuck itself out a few inches into the void. He tied one end of the rope around it with a knot his father had taught him and then he dropped the tangle and watched it unwind, the far end striking the dusty ground with an audible slap ten seconds later. A mythical snake.

Taking a series of deep breaths, Ug abruptly pushed himself into space and dangled. His large hands clutched the sinew and burned as they slid down and for a terrifying moment he thought he wouldn't be able to stop himself from sliding all the way to the bottom at a speed comparable to a fall. He gripped tighter and braked slightly.

Then he worked out that if he wrapped one of his legs around the rope, he could control his descent even more accurately. He passed the level of Og and snarled at him. Og jerked his head up with a frown but Ug already was below him, the pain of his blisters truly forgotten in the swelling and joyful fury of triumph that suffused his being.

His feet struck the ground with a force that jarred the bones in his hips and he keeled over, grimacing through the agony until it began to fade, to become a comfortable ache, like a frost burn.

The sun flared high overhead. That huge yellow ball had

been in a bad mood lately, flinging arcs of fire over itself. Ug could almost hear the sun hissing in the sky as it cast shadows with very sharp definition from every solid object, including himself as he stood up.

He bunched his fists and waited for Og to reach the ground.

"Ra-Kel!" screamed Ug in anticipation.

"Ug!" she responded as she came lower, still on the left shoulder of an ugly brute, a treacherous rival, a predator…

Og jumped the final few feet, landing upright.

Ug bared his teeth and charged.

To Ug's amazement, Og didn't brace himself to absorb the impact but turned and ran. He was fleet of foot, even with a woman on his shoulder, and easily outpaced his pursuer. Ug was vaguely aware of the entrance to a cave at the base of the mesa that passed in a blur as he forced himself to increase his speed. He howled in frustration.

But his ululation achieved nothing.

Og didn't race off across the plain but circled the massive outcrop, the mighty cliff, keeping close to the root of the sandy rock. Panting, Ug held his aching side and found his vision blurring.

But he didn't give up. He bit his lip, tasted blood.

The sun beat down in boiling waves.

Sweat made Ug's eyes smart, as if nettle juice had been squeezed into them, and he wiped both with a hairy forearm. He staggered, the bloated bursting sun seeming to pulse inside his head. Loops of fire leapt from the surface of that relentless orb, chiding tongues of unbearable energy. With a sickening gasp, Ug turned the next corner.

He had completely circled the mesa…

Back to the spot where he had descended, and Og was waiting for him, and so was Ra-Kel, but the result was hideous.

Og had made a noose from the end of the long sinew, the rope that Ug had used to descend from the top of the cliff, and had placed it around the neck of Ra-Kel. He was holding the woman up in his burly arms and Ug knew that if he let her go, Ra-Kel would hang.

Ug didn't know what to do. If he attacked Og, then his woman would choke to death. If he ran to help her, Og would take the opportunity to kill him while he was distracted. He stood still.

But Og made the decision for him. He let Ra-Kel go.

Her scream was cut off, turned into a gargle as the noose tightened and she dangled in mid-air, her feet a few inches above the ground. Og moved aside and beckoned at Ug, mouthing obscenities. Ug ran at him like a bull and Og danced nimbly aside, laughing.

He was standing near the entrance to that other cave, Og was, and with his hands on his hips he was grinning at Ug, mocking him, while Ra-Kel kicked ineffectually in her death throes.

Then something large rushed out of the cave.

A bear! The bear from above...

Ug was sure it was the same beast that he had chased out of the egg. It must have climbed safely down the cliff, using its claws to grip the stone, moving into this new home, making a life for itself here; but always ready to take revenge on humans, those who had evicted it, persecuted it, hurt it with the sharp edges of broken pebbles.

Og didn't have time to turn, to see what form his death had taken. The bear broke his neck with a single swipe.

Ug ran to help Ra-Kel. Then the sun stopped spitting.

Everything lurched, faded, congealed.

The sinew snapped. Ra-Kel sprawled to the ground, to the sidewalk, a pavement of neatly fitting slabs. Ug crouched over her. "Are you alright? I think the sunstorm has finished now..."

Ug remembered the way things really were.

The mesa was a skyscraper. An experimental rocket had landed on the flat roof and the chimp inside had managed to open the capsule hatch and escape. Here it was now, lurking in the shadows of the lobby entrance. It made a series of rude gestures at Ug.

The parachute fabric, the cords attaching it to the capsule. Everything had been interpreted differently, hadn't it? The chimp had been a bear. It wasn't possible, was it? Just because a violent solar storm had jammed all the communications satellites in orbit...

The man on the ground stood and dusted off his suit.

"Oglethorpe!" bellowed Ug.

"Yes, it's me. The solar storm is over."

"It was a quick Stone Age, thank goodness. I suppose we'd better get back to work now," said Mr Ugolino.

Mr Oglethorpe nodded. They both glanced at Raquel.

She rubbed her bruised throat.

"We ought to file a report about this too."

"Later. The accounts take priority. The auditors are arriving tomorrow and there can't be any irregularities."

She nodded. Then she squinted. "Was it painful?"

"Being killed by a bear? You bet!"

They went inside the building and took the elevator to the top floor. A mammoth that was slow to change back lumbered past them in the widest corridor, knocking over the water cooler.

> "The sun regularly has Earth-sized storms on its surface that end up ejecting dangerous radiation and particles into space. Mostly these dangerous bits of energy head off into deep space. But what would happen if the Earth got in the way? You could kiss goodbye to the Internet and your electricity supply. Banks and governments would not be able to function. Satellites would be blinded." – *The Doomsday Handbook*

The Anvil Cloud

I made the dreadful mistake of parachuting into an anvil cloud. I won't try to justify my decision. It was simply wrong.

They are mature thunderstorm clouds and are like sacks of thunder, rain, hail and wind, and they look just like anvils that are boiling furiously. The air inside them goes round in an endless loop.

People with a scientific interest in the weather prefer to call these clouds *cumulonimbus incus* because it shows they are more professional than ordinary folks like me and that's fair enough really.

Anything that gets stuck in one can end up going up and down for a long time. Maybe the forces in the cloud will tear the thing apart, maybe they won't. There's no way of predicting the outcome.

Aircraft have been devoured by them whole.

I jumped out of my own aeroplane before I knew any of this. My canopy opened and I descended through the cloud, icy water lashing my face and blue lightning frazzling my nerves, and I was astonished to meet another parachutist coming back up. We passed each other.

"Hey!" I shouted.

"Hey!" he called back.

"What are you doing here? Did you get stuck?"

"Yes, an hour back..."

And then we were out of earshot. I kept falling through the chaos of cold and noise, through the wind and the thunder, and then just before I popped out of the base of the cloud, I felt myself stopping, reversing direction, going back up, lifted by malicious currents of air.

And I met the man again, for he was coming down.

"Hello once more!" I cried.

"Good afternoon. Goodbye! See you soon!"

We passed each other.

I continued to rise, but then to my bewilderment I met him again higher up. He was descending and I was still ascending and this situation didn't make any sense. "Hey you!" I bellowed.

"Long time, no see," he shouted back.

"It *can't* be you. That's impossible. To fall down you have to go back to the top and I passed you just now."

"Very well, I admit it. I'm his twin brother."

"What a mean trick to play!"

He shrugged and then he was gone. I reached the top of the cloud and my head actually poked out of the top of it and into the blue sky and I drank deep of the serenity and sanity it afforded.

But then I began dropping back into the nightmare.

As I plunged I soon saw him coming back up. He grinned. "It does get a bit boring in here. That's why I lied."

"I think I understand," I answered, but I didn't.

He went his way, I went mine.

Then his brother came up to pass me. "Hello."

"I think it's inappropriate."

"Don't be such a prig!" he chided me.

We left each other and I continued to fall. But then I saw him again and he was coming up, not down. And—

"I just want to apologise for the misunderstanding."

I was aghast. "Fine, fine!"

"No, it's not fine. We have been cruel to you."

"I think your apology is the joke. I am getting wise to such games now. I don't believe you are him *or* his brother."

"True. We are triplets, not twins. It does happen."

I grimaced and passed him.

Then I reached the bottom of the cloud and started going back up. There was nothing I wanted more now than to be alone. Strange! You'd think a man in my position would crave company.

Not me. I was ashamed of my species.

Inanimate objects seemed nobler than human beings.

And there *were* other things stuck in that anvil cloud, not just a brace of foolish parachutists, but toy balloons, kites, newspapers, the broken branches of trees, books, bottles, cardigans, bags.

The first brother came down and waved cheerily.

I ignored him. And the second.

I also ignored the third.

But then I met a fourth and when he shouted, "Nice day for it, what?" I found myself responding against my will.

"What sort of mother did you have, all of you?"

"She did her level best."

I chewed my lip but he continued, "Yes, times were hard, but we never went without, not one of the four of us went hungry or cold. She was that kind of woman. A survivor and fighter."

I felt a little melancholy after this encounter. Should I have tried harder to live and let live, to be accepting?

I reached the bottom of the cloud, started going back up.

And five brothers passed me.

I couldn't take any more of this. It was mockery of the worst sort, of the numerical kind, and I felt like drowning myself in the rain, but I knew it would be too difficult to do that, and that I was doomed to remain in my harness and go up and down, down and up, until I became a skeleton, my bones not really connected to each other but simply moving all together at the same rate, so the illusion of an integral structure was preserved.

Then I suddenly saw something that gave me hope.

A curious sort of hope.

Black hope, if you can imagine such a thing.

It was another anvil cloud.

A smaller anvil cloud but exquisite in its own way, which had somehow got trapped inside the bigger one.

I seized my chance and pulled the strings of my parachute and steered myself into it. Thus I got stuck a second time, stuck within stuckness, and up and down I went but *inside* the outer up and down, so that sometimes I was going up while the new cloud that enveloped me was going down and I guess that my speed relative to the ground was zero. That was a comforting thought and I allowed it to comfort me a lot.

Inside the second anvil cloud was a third.

Triplets? I had to enter it.

The mathematics and physics of my movements was now getting more complicated and would continue to do so when I entered the fourth, fifth and sixth clouds, and all the others there might be. The further I got away from the brothers, the better. But eventually the final anvil cloud would only be as big as my body. It would fit me like a shroud and I wouldn't be able to move up and down at all inside it. I would be stuck immobile while all the innumerable ups and downs went on around me.

Then I might be able to paddle the cloud sideways and out of the muddle into freedom. A long journey but worthwhile. I just had to extend my arms and poke them out on either side and flap them gently, swimming like a man who thinks he's a fish that thinks it's a bird.

And that's what I did.

I even got home safe, which is where I am now.

Drinking hot chocolate, and wiping my lips on the silk of my parachute, and staring out the window into the street.

Women with very large bellies sometimes walk past.

How many brothers inside each one?

Stuck in a womb, rotating, passing each other.

The only way you'll ever get me back in one of those anvil clouds is if I'm completely hammered. That's no joke.

The Apple of My Sky

Why don't adults ever climb trees for fun? They climb mountains and cliffs and no one thinks it odd, not even if they get stuck halfway up, but the moment a grown man or woman is found helpless in a tall oak or elm then it's a reason for mirth. Children are permitted to scale trees, and so are cats, but never adults, unless they have serious reasons for doing so, including the rescue of those offspring and pets. How unfair!

Those were the thoughts that passed through the feverish head of Mummery Tumble as he lay on his back on the spacious balcony of his Kleine Scheidegg hotel room. The hotel staff had been thoughtful enough to move his bed out into the fresh air and the view of the Alps before him filled him with both joy and melancholy, for although he appreciated the magnificence of the vista he was also frustrated by his inability to engage with it in physical terms.

"Curse this leg!" he sighed, as he regarded his bandaged limb.

The previous day, while on a simple stroll, his bag of apples had split and the fruit had rolled under his feet, sending him crashing awkwardly to the ground and causing a bone to break. So now his climbing holiday was over and he was reduced to immobility, frowned down upon by those immense icy giants that he still dreamed of befriending; for Mummery rarely conquered peaks, preferring to work *with* them.

Sighing for the thousandth time this morning, he placed his eye to the lens of the telescope that had been set up on a tripod next to his bed. As he scanned the face of the Eiger, adjusting focus, looking for climbers in order to monitor their progress with a mixture of envy and displaced pride, he suddenly stiffened in amazement. He removed his eye, blinked it furiously, returned it to the lens. No, he hadn't been deceived by an optical illusion. This was real.

It was a tree. A tree climbing the mountain!

But how was such a totally unexpected thing possible?

Trees don't move, or rather they move exceedingly slowly, pushing their roots through the soil, reaching out to touch the clouds with their branches; they certainly never scale difficult peaks with such fluidity and strength. This particular tree was clinging to precarious handholds and footholds with the tips of its twigs and roots but it had a confident posture, leaning back and refusing to hug the rock. Up it went, more efficiently than a human could.

Was it alone? No, it was roped to another tree on a lower ledge. The rope in question was a thick vine and the second tree was paying it out carefully, braced to absorb the shock of a fall. Mummery returned his attention to the leading tree. Something moved in its highest branches. What might it be? A minor adjustment of the focus revealed it to be a man with a basket picking apples! This was simply too much. How could the fellow be so blasé?

"I bet he doesn't realise what has happened!" Mummery exclaimed. "He merely climbed a tree to pick some apples and while he was doing so the tree uprooted itself and came here to tackle this mountain. It's the same as a man who unwittingly carries a spider to the summit in his pocket. But this tree is making very rapid progress. The fellow with the basket is going to have a real shock when he descends and finds himself standing on top of the Eigerwand!"

A few months later, when his leg had perfectly healed, Mummery was invited to join an expedition by his colleague Whymper Bowman. The plan was to ascend a gigantic apple that had appeared overnight, falling out of a clear sky, perhaps from a distant star, onto the city of New York. It had impaled itself neatly on a number of skyscrapers and had become an accepted feature of the urban skyline. Engineers had even bored subway tunnels through it so that trains could rumble the pips.

But it had never been climbed. Mummery and Whymper boarded a steamer and crossed the Atlantic and when they entered the harbour and passed the Statue of Liberty they were overawed. "The Big Apple!" breathed Mummery, to which Whymper responded, "Yes, and over there is the big apple!" Truly it was enormous, a shiny red apple as crisp as autumn itself, noble and imposing but also homely; the pipedream of a demented orchard-keeper, turned into unabashed reality.

They disembarked and approached the base of the succulent mountain. On the northern side the skin was slightly more wrinkled and would favour toeholds and fingertip grips, so they attacked the ascent from that direction. The crampons that Whymper fitted to his boots were of a radical new design and Mummery questioned them. "Crampons? No, they are peelers. I intend to peel the apple as I go up it," Whymper said, "in the name of science of course!"

Mummery wondered what the name of science was but he didn't even hazard a guess at this juncture.

Finally attaining the summit of the monstrous fruit, they shook hands and frowned at the gathering clouds of an approaching storm. Were there apple trees somewhere up there? Anything was possible providing it wasn't a self-contradiction, Mummery told himself.

On yet another continent, he found himself travelling in a train full of drunken people. Someone shouted that an impromptu cabaret had started in the buffet car and there was a stampede towards it. A hand gripped his shoulder and a voice asked, "Aren't you coming?" Mummery blinked up at a familiar face. It was the fellow who had stood in the branches of the apple tree! "I know who you are. I know that you piggybacked your way to the apex of the Eiger," he declared.

The man laughed and nodded. "My name is Wockycough Riptidy, but you may call me Mr Science."

So that was the answer to the riddle…

Mummery said, "I prefer to remain here in my seat. I'm not a drunkard or a reveller. I like the peace and serenity of the remotest regions of the planet. That's my kind of entertainment."

Mr Science leaned forward and whispered, "Then we understand each other perfectly. That's also how I feel. Let me make a confession." He fumbled in his pocket and drew out a piece of paper that he folded many times and presented to his new friend. Mummery took it with a frown. It looked more like a unicorn than a confession to him. He popped it in his mouth.

"I arranged the cabaret in order to get the passengers crammed tightly into one small space," continued Mr Science. "They are mostly influential young executives. I plan to embark on an expedition right here. It will involve some difficult social climbing. Do you want to join me? Social climbing is much more challenging than rock climbing."

Mummery nodded without needing to hesitate, then he stood and accompanied Mr Science to the buffet car. It was crammed with sweating enthusiasts of the performance that was taking place at the far end, where an apple tree danced and shed its leaves one by one. "A striptrees!" shouted Mr Science and when Mummery called back, "Surely you mean strip*tease*?" he was greeted by laughter. "Put these on," said Mr Science, giving Mummery a pair of odd crampons.

"Juicers?" wondered Mummery as he held them up and examined them. But Mr Science was already strapping his own to his boots and setting off, climbing over the apple-cheeked youths with determination and confidence. So Mummery followed with a spider in his pocket.

The Taste of Turtle Tears

There are certain kinds of butterfly that live exclusively on the tears of other animals. Even butterflies that like to drink nectar will still often alight on the cheeks of a beast that has been weeping.

There is nothing illogical in this action really, for the butterflies crave salt, and tears are one of the richest sources of sodium. Butterflies that dwell near the sea don't need to do this because the wind is already laden with salt and the wind sprinkles it over the flowers.

But butterflies that have their homes far inland will usually find that the salt the wind can carry has been shed long before it reaches them, so they will be desperately short of the vital mineral.

Deep in the Amazon rainforest, far from the ocean, there are flotillas of butterflies that have become specialised tear-drinkers. It may seem a gloomy feast for such a beautiful creature but what choice do they have? Without salt death is certain and a slow agonising death too.

So they find it essential that larger animals cry; and one way to ensure a regular supply of tears is to encourage these animals to shed them; and the best way of doing that it to make them feel sad.

How on earth do butterflies make other animals sad?

In one small region of that mighty jungle some butterflies have learned a few things that butterflies elsewhere have yet to learn. They know that the tears of the yellow-spotted river turtle are the saltiest and most nourishing of all, and they also know how to speak turtle language.

Actually, this last part isn't quite true. They don't *speak* the language but write it instead, in mid air, with their fluttering bodies. The orange and yellow butterflies form words in the turtle tongue that tell extremely sad stories and the turtles read them and burst into racking sobs.

The butterflies don't need to form individual letters to make the words of a sentence because the written language of these turtles isn't alphabetical but pictographic. Each symbol stands for one word. This fortunately means it takes less butterflies to tell a turtle tale than it otherwise might. There is a limit to the number of butterflies that can drink the tears of a single turtle. Having said this, there have been occasions when more than one turtle arrived to experience the sad story that was being related for them.

One memorable afternoon the butterflies had an audience of no less than six turtles, but more than one is a rarity. The stories that make turtles cry aren't especially sophisticated. Simple tragic narratives suffice. Accounts of brave but foolish turtles that ended up as meals for jaguars; doomed loved affairs; stories about ungrateful children being mean to their mother; bitter ironies about what happens to naive turtles in the big bad world.

When the turtles can bear no more, they begin to weep and then it's time for the butterflies to land and take a drink. The turtle tears give the insects the salt they need and they taste great too. The only problem is that the sadness, or at least some of it, comes with the substance.

Yes, it's true. A little of the morose feeling is transferred into every tear, so the butterflies generally feel rather sad themselves afterwards. For the turtle the weeping might be cathartic but not so for the butterflies. They just feel sad without any emotional cleansing of the soul.

One day it occurred to the butterflies that tears are not only produced by sadness. They wondered if they might switch to telling funny stories so that the turtles would cry with laughter. Worth a try!

A comedy that will appeal to a turtle is no more polished than a tragedy that will fill it with melancholy. Turtles like farces best, with lots of characters narrowly avoiding each other in complicated love triangles. The butterflies told these stories and the turtles wept with joy.

These tears tasted sweeter than the juice of sadness.

But they were a little *too* sweet.

The butterflies enjoyed them nonetheless, but one morning, while sunning themselves on the river bank, among the flowers they held a discussion. Tragic tears were too bitter, comic tears too sweet. Might a way be found to combine and moderate the two flavours into something better? Was there such a thing as *tragicomedy*, a blend of both genres?

They weren't sure but they decided to try anyway.

The next story they told was a masterpiece of plotting and it manipulated the emotions of the turtle who witnessed it in a way that previously would have seemed implausible, swooping from the black depths of despair to the dizzy heights of mirth and back again at a velocity that to a turtle must have seemed horrifying and exhilarating at the same time.

The subsequent tears of tragicomedy were rated very highly. Indeed the butterflies considered them utterly perfect.

They began to tour their performance across the entire region and back to the starting point. It might be supposed they could simply have moved to a new home closer to the sea, where salt would have been plentiful, but the home they already had was far from meddling humans and had its advantages. Why should they emigrate? They liked it here and now that they had the recipe for the best tears ever tasted, there was no more need to worry.

But giving the same performance day after day meant that they became a little complacent. They put less effort into forming the words correctly. If one of the butterflies was late to get into position the others would go ahead without him or her. Yes, their work became sloppy.

And one awful day the turtle that was the sole audience member started laughing in a different way from usual. The butterflies carried on and, when the turtle cried, they abandoned the story and took their drink. But the flavour was off this time, very peculiar, and mildly toxic.

It didn't kill the butterflies but it made their souls sick for a few days and in that time they squabbled with each other or drooped their wings pathetically while resting on petals or muttered dark ideas about self destruction or found it impossible to go to sleep. They were depressed.

The problem is that the last performance had been a disaster. So casual had the butterflies become, so cavalier with their theatrical duties, that most of them hadn't bothered to make neat symbols in the air. The pictographs were ragged and badly formed. As a consequence, the *meaning* of the words of the story had changed. It had become gibberish.

And yes, the turtle had laughed and wept, but not because of catharsis or amusement. No, he had guffawed and cried in derision, in contempt, his tears and laughter directed *at* the butterflies rather than *with* them. These tears were pure poison, not strong enough to kill the insects but certainly potent enough to make them feel very bad about themselves.

The solution was to forget about amateur dramatics.

And now the butterflies have a highly organised and superbly disciplined troupe of *professional* actors who give daily shows down by the river. They are even building a special venue there, an open air amphitheatre, though how they are doing this with their little thin legs is beyond my knowing; and the actors in this troupe are never sloppy or slapdash.

It remains to be seen if butterfly theatre ever catches on in that isolated part of the forest. I sincerely hope it does.

Their plan is to make everything as honest as possible, so the old idea of tricking the turtles into weeping is now considered a bit vulgar. A more ethical alternative has been proposed, that the price of admission for a show should be set at two tears, one from each eye, payable after the performance; and only if the show has the desired emotional impact.

The Musical Universe

"The idea of the oscillating universe has finally been discredited and I'm rather glad about that," said Dr Wombat as he left the university building through the doors of an obscure rear exit.

Perry Crammer, his favourite research student, followed him with one of his affable shrugs, a shrug that wouldn't have been seen by his myopic mentor, even if he had been facing the right way. "It was discredited years ago, really; but now we're *sure* our cosmos is fated to keep on expanding and expanding."

"The process is accelerating."

"Quite right," muttered Dr Wombat.

"But," said Perry, moistening his lips with his precocious tongue. "I don't understand why this fact should have any emotional impact on you at all. The scale of events is too grand in space and time to influence our little human lives. So why are you glad?"

Dr Wombat opened an iron gate in a wall and stepped through into the quiet ambience of a cobbled alleyway in the adjacent historic quarter of the town. This was where the tourists should have gone, but never did. It was kept a secret from them. Mainly students frequented the labyrinthine ways, the quaint cafés and secluded parks.

"A universe that expands to a certain size, and then contracts to a point, before blasting outwards again, and so on forever; reminds me too much of one of those damn musical instruments, the wheezy kind. What are the horrid objects called? Accordions, is it?"

"Or concertinas," ventured Perry.

"Yes, yes! I hate the sound they make. I loathe the thought that maybe the universe sounds like one of them."

"But this is all a bit fanciful," chuckled Perry.

Dr Wombat said nothing in reply. He turned corners and passed under the awnings of shops, his face now in shadow, then in sunlight, so that he resembled an archaic thinking machine with flashing bulbs pushed to the limits of its ability.

Then he boomed:

"I know a little place that's perfect for lunch!"

And turning the next corner he stopped at a café and turned his head to beam at Perry; but even as a smile began to curl on his lips, a frown was furrowing his brow. On an elevated platform, next to the tables and chairs of the cute establishment, a band was playing music. Many musicians and many instruments and one of them was—

"An accordion! Blast it!" bellowed Dr Wombat.

"No, it's a concertina," said Perry.

"Let's find somewhere else to eat. I can't possibly munch a salad, and slurp a coffee, and ogle a waitress with that din rattling around in my ears. It sounds like an asthmatic donkey that has gone mad. I can't understand why the management thought it made business sense to book them. Very few people like this kind of cacophony."

"Well, to be perfectly candid, I enjoy the other instruments that are in the hands of the other musicians," said Perry.

"I suppose they are agreeable but the accordion spoils everything. Do you understand now why I'm so emphatic that we don't live in a universe that undergoes an eternal cycle of inflation and deflation? Honk, wheeze and drone! A nightmarish appetite suppressant! Come, I know plenty of other cafés, alternatives to this one. Hurry up!"

But Perry was still listening, tapping his foot to the tune.

Then he glanced at his mentor and saw the expression of disapproval etched there and sought to explain himself. "I'm filtering out the sound of the concertina with my mind. It's the sound of the blampet that I love. I'll come in a minute. I took blampet lessons."

"I suppose the blampet is acceptable. I am willing to declare the flutes, trumpets, trombones, banjos, chimes and fiddles to also be inoffensive. It is simply the accordion that I can't stand."

"Concertina," said Perry in a very quiet voice. "Listen!"

And he pointed at the blampet player.

The musician in question held a blampet at arm's length. The string of the thing dangled down. Then he reached out with his free hand to tug the string and the blampet popped and let loose a sweet but powerful note. He was clearly a virtuoso because he delved into a bucket and procured yet another blampet without skipping a beat; and the tempo of this music was now very fast. Perry sighed with pleasure.

"It's a superb instrument, one of my favourites. And you know what? I would say that it's a very good model of our universe, the real cosmos we happen to live in. After all, that's what the new results from our telescope prove, isn't it? Our universe will expand and expand until, eventually, one day in the unimaginably remote future—"

Dr Wombat finished his sentence for him. "It pops."

They waited for the musician to play another note on the blampet, but finally the concertina's croaking proved too much for old Dr Wombat; he plucked Perry's sleeve and dragged him along the alley and around new corners to a café that was silent and almost as quaint. They ordered salads and espresso and munched in satisfaction.

When the meal was done, Perry wiped his lips with a napkin and he became philosophical, as he always did with a full stomach. "Suppose we are living in just one universe out of many?"

"Ah, the multiverse conjecture. What of it?" Dr Wombat smiled as he slurped the dregs of his cup. He felt indulgent.

"Well, it could be that each universe resembles a different instrument, a different *musical* instrument I mean. We don't exist in a universe that is like a concertina, true, but one that's awfully similar to a blampet. What if other universes in some parallel spacetime act more like flutes, trumpets, trombones, banjos, chimes and fiddles?"

Dr Wombat folded his arms, sat back in his chair, laughed.

"I just hope the melody is synchronised."

Perry also laughed. "But seriously, a universe that resembles a banjo. Imagine that! Would the laws of physics even be the same? Probably not! I enjoy all this wild speculation, you see."

"Post-lunch prattlings. Harmless," said Dr Wombat.

An odd light appeared in Perry's eyes.

"In some of those other universes the musical instruments themselves might be different. I don't know how workable that makes my analogy. I bet in some of those alternative realities they don't have blampets or even know what they are. Can you credit that?"

Dr Wombat rotated his head as a waitress walked past with a wiggle. Then he answered, "That's going too far."

The men got up to depart and return to the university.

The Bones of Jones

I am lying on my back.

The truth is that I'm on my front.

That's how easy it is for me to tell a lie when I am on my back. With no real effort, I can assert, quite convincingly, that I'm on my front and people are more likely to believe me than not.

I like to lie on my back. It's my favourite position for lying.

My chin is made of wood.

I keep a miniature pig in a jar on a shelf.

That shelf is wooden and the wood came from my chin.

My face is much shorter now.

See what I mean? Lies, all lies. They rolled off my tongue like spherical giraffes on an extremely steep incline.

No, not at all like that...

I don't try hard to lie when I'm on my back. It comes naturally. I suspect it's something to do with magnetism, with the circulation of the molten iron that I use as a substitute for spinal fluid.

Having said that, I can also lie competently in many other positions. I'm not a pun trick pony, like Hayley Jude, who can only fib when she's in a stable condition. Hayley, or Hay as everybody calls her, can't lie unless she is utterly motionless, her muscles rigid, her breathing as shallow as it possibly can be, her pulse rate as low as a midget-diver.

I bet you didn't know divers are used to explore midgets?

They aren't, as a matter of fact.

And Hayley Jude doesn't exist, I made her up, but only after she turned me down. Brutally. That's what I do.

And it's what she does too. Hay Jude.

Lying on my back, as I am, I can see the ceiling.

Seeing the ceiling is soothing.

This is because the ceiling is so high above me it might as well be a sky, but the sky of another world, a paradise planet in orbit around some other star, a daydream made real, a private heaven.

Utopia. Itopia. Wetopia.

The constellations have been painted on with luminous paint and how do they sparkle, you ask? Like low energy chemical reactions, that's how, in other words exactly like what they are, rendering the simile redundant. Luckily it took voluntary redundancy, that simile.

The telephone rings... I turn my head to look.

I can't recall why I put rings on it. The necklaces and bracelets are also a mystery. I must have thought it needed adornment when I was younger, but that was a mistake. It was fine as it was.

It doesn't work anymore. The metal jewellery interferes with the circuits and makes them malfunction badly.

No, it makes them malfunction well. If the malfunction was bad it would be a low quality malfunction and the telephone would probably still work, but it doesn't. It is merely a dead ornament.

Too bad. I hate talking to people I can't see anyway. How do I know they aren't pulling baboon faces, parading in underpants, frying plantains in bicycle oil on dangerous stoves? Too risky.

A star falls from the distant ceiling. A meteor.

It grows bigger as it approaches me and then I realise that it's not really a meteor but a parachute with a badly fashioned ball hanging from it. The ball is a piece of paper that has been scrunched up.

Clearly it's a message from my employers.

They can reach me anywhere.

And I'm always on duty.

The message lands on my chest and the parachute canopy, which is just a pocket handkerchief, settles over my face.

Snot funny. So I blow my nose in it contemptuously.

Then I fling it aside so I can see.

And now that I can see, I am in a position to turn the paper ball into a flat page again and read what is written.

Dear Corker,

> *Hope this finds you well or, if not well, then adequate; or. if not adequate, then bearable; or, if not bearable, then vicious.*
>
> *It has recently come to our attention that the bones of a man by the name of Jones, who drowned a few years ago, have started telling the most appalling lies. His bones lie under the sea and the physical and moral shockwaves caused by these lies are causing a hazard to shipping. As our specialist Lie Detector we want you to do something or anything about it.*
>
> *Will you do something, or anything about it; pretty please?*
>
> *If you refuse we will slaughter you.*
>
> *But it's entirely your decision. Cheerio, buster!*

Grillchin and the Team

What could I do? One doesn't refuse Grillchin. I knew an agent once who refused him and that *agent* is now *a gent* instead, which sounds rather nice, but the insertion of that space between the 'a' and the 'g' of his identity was painful in the extreme and he never recovered.

So I sigh deeply, because that's the correct way to sigh when one has to prepare for a voyage under the sea, and I turn on my side and reach out with my hand to punch the buttons of the bedside unit.

Punching them makes me feel better, but not much, so little in fact that it makes me feel worse, my knuckles anyway...

Then I press them properly, with my fingertips, and those buttons activate a motor inside my mattress which propels my bed on numerous little wheels out of my bedroom to a destination specified by the sequence of buttons I selected. A perfect system for men who like to lie in bed, and only marginally less so for men who prefer to be honest under the sheets.

The bed accelerates steadily, passes out of the house, doors opening and closing automatically to ease its passage, and now it is on the street, joining the flow of traffic, moving at an incredible speed.

I take cover under the duvet as the wind generated by my velocity ruffles my hair unpleasantly. Also I wish to hide from the stares and honks of ordinary vehicles and their passengers, who are unused to being overtaken by a bedstead. But soon I leave the city and find myself on a quieter road leading to the secret beach where my private harbour is located.

The bed bounces over the shingles and the motor grumbles when we get onto the sand. However, without any serious problems, it deposits me next to the jetty that I use to moor my entire ocean-going fleet.

For I have many craft that ply the waters of the deep blue yonder. I have yachts, schooners, clippers, galleons, caravels, longboats, catamarans, canoes, barges, galleys, yawls, hulks, cobles, dinghies, feluccas, cutters, dhows, junks, gondolas, sampans, punts, skiffs, and trawlers.

Unluckily, they were all bashed together during a stupendous tempest, and the hulls interpenetrated each other, and the whole thing is such a knot of vessels that it can't be undone. So, when I put to sea, I do so simultaneously in every one, and it's certainly an odd sight to witness Captain Corker strolling the deck(s) of that maritime mix-up, like a mini-minotaur in a maze.

But today, I need to dive below the waves, not swish over them, so it is to my submarine that I'm headed. I only have one submarine but it's a good one. It was given to me by an inventor called Boppo Higgins and it is fast and reliable, quite roomy too; and, most importantly, very watertight. I jump out of bed, stroll along the jetty to where this machine waits, and climb down the ladder into the cockpit, which I seal by shutting a transparent plastic dome on a hinge over it. I pull levers and twist knobs and press buttons.

And so I'm off, heading for the seabed where the bones of Jones are lying, and thinking how terrible it is when bones avoid the truth. Why do they do that? Is it because the word *fibia* nearly sounds like *fibber*? But the word *metatarsal* nearly sounds like *sent a parcel* and no bone has ever worked successfully as a postman in my extensive and expensive experience, or even outside it. I regard it as an unsolvable mystery and maybe it regards me the same way. It would serve me right if it did. I like being served right.

In such cases, the waiter is efficient and puts every dish in its proper place and bows deeply before wishing me *bon appétit*. Better to be served *right* than served wrong, which means being *left* with a service so rotten you twiddle your fork and spoon until they rust and the spaghetti never arrives. I am lucky never to have supped in such restaurants. I would still be there if I had, waiting for the meal, until the future itself became the pasta.

But none of that is important. It's far more pertinent to say that, within the hour, I arrived at the precise spot where the bones of Jones were. I imagined they would be scattered randomly but, in fact, they had been arranged in a neat circle; too perfect a shape for the artistry of the currents to have fashioned. They were telling new lies even as I approached...

"I am a renowned opera singer," said a femur.

"Scotland was put on the world upside down," said the maxilla.

"Two plus two equals five," said the sphenoid.

"Love is half an onion," said a phalange.

"One quarter," corrected the coccyx.

"I can't talk," said the mandible.

"Chairs are used as currency in Yuckystan," said an ulna.

"Griffins are monkeys in disguise," said one of the cervical vertebrae, to which another responded, "Swans dwell in nests of solid yogurt." But the first objected to this, "Swans don't exist at all!"

"Squeezed coughs think like weasels," said the scapula.

"Chums are hexagonal," said an astragalus.

"Jokes are always unfunny," chuckled the humerus.

"Gloves knit themselves," said the patella.

"Diameters hate cheese," said a radius.

"Unless it's in a pi," countered the ischium.

"Glue is pear cider," said the clavicle.

And so on. It was very disturbing and I was disturbed.

The submarine designed for me by Boppo Higgins has lots of prehensile tentacles and mechanical arms that I can control from the cockpit, and there are signalling devices that enable me to communicate with anything on the outside in a myriad of practical and impractical ways.

I can, for instance, shoot beautifully scripted letters enclosed in tungsten canisters for the recipient to read at their leisure, once they have recovered from being struck on the noggin by the things.

Or I can make the hands on the ends of the arms perform sign language in known and lost tongues, and, it goes without saying, that I can broadcast sound at any volume and frequency I might desire.

I had decided on this occasion to send my messages to Jones with the aid of a large xylophone that extends from the prow of the vessel, which happens to be shaped like a gigantic head, incidentally.

The xylophone juts like a callous sneer from the mouth.

For some strange reason, bones and xylophones instinctively understand each other. I fiddled with the necessary controls and one of the mechanical arms played a nice little melody on the instrument.

This melody said, "Why don't you cease your untrue chatter and try to be more respectable in future, you bones! Don't you appreciate the atrocious havoc you are playing with the serenity of the sea?"

Then I played a few more notes and these notes said:

"You are upsetting the fish, whales, coral reefs and all the other entities in the surrounding waters. Also, you are spooking the crews of merchant ships that pass overhead; for the vibrations of your lies pass through the hulls and into the dreams of sleeping sailors and when those sailors awake they believe things that can never be. For example: that the moon grew from a seed planted in a very big garden, or that ants are driven by clockwork."

I continued playing notes on the xylophone and the gist of my words was that bones should rest in peace, or at least tell the truth if they really felt they had to speak, and that I, Pop Corker (that's my full name), had no intention of letting the bones of *my* skeleton behave so despicably.

At last they answered me.

"We never lie," they chorused.

"*That* is the biggest lie of all, you liars!" I tinkled.

They shrugged metaphorically.

Before I could say or do anything more my submarine was rocked by a sudden disruption in the water around me. Some object was approaching at an unadvisable velocity. The bones seemed to be full of trepidation and I craned my neck in the cockpit, struggling to see through the bubble what might be the cause of the shockwave. Then it appeared.

It was a diver in a bulky suit riding a sledge pulled by more than a dozen seadogs. He swooped low and skimmed the seabed and yanked the reins just in time, halting his crazy rush inches from the circle of bones. Then he dismounted and strode with slow motion strides into the centre of the circle of bones, where he kneeled and began playing with them.

I frowned. No, he wasn't really playing. He was picking them up one at a time and repositioning them, making the circle slightly smaller, contracting it so that it covered a lesser area of the seabed.

The bones remained silent during this procedure.

Either he hadn't noticed my submarine, or else he had deliberately chosen to ignore it, so I xylophoned a protest.

"What do you think you are doing? Unhand those bones!"

Without rising from his knees, or even glancing back over his shoulder, he laughed while continuing with his work.

The sensitive microphone on my hull picked up his subsequent words and relayed them to me. "No, I won't stop. I am an artist and this is my art. You are obviously a barbarian if you want to prevent me from finishing this masterpiece. I dive down every day and make the circle of bones smaller by a tiny amount. It is my art and I am an artist. So there!"

I paled at once, for I recognised the voice.

"Grillchin!" I barely whispered.

"Yes," he said, indicating with a nod of his head the seadogs, "and that is the Team." He must have had his own microphone and amplifier to hear what I had said. But he wasn't angry with me.

Then I realised the incongruity of the situation.

"It was you who asked me to investigate these bones in the first place and stop them from further lying!" I cried.

"Of course. Why shouldn't I? I don't want them telling fibs when they are fated to be merely the component parts of a superb artwork. I gave you the task of preventing them from lying, nothing else. Plus good art really needs someone to view it to make it complete. That's the other reason I wanted you here. At the moment it's only a work in progress though."

"What exactly does it mean?" I wailed. "Because the continual shrinking of a circle of bones, or indeed a circle of any kind, seems a pointless exercise. I have nothing against conceptual art and yet—"

"A pointless exercise?" he roared. "On the contrary, Corker dear boy, you are utterly wrong. *I am making a point.*"

I tried to laugh but no sound emerged from my mouth, and I had forgotten the xylophone equivalent of a chuckle. A circle that steadily contracts will end as a point of no dimensions, of course.

"What would Jones say about this?" I finally managed.

"That's none of your business. Just be grateful you have a chin made out of wood rather than iron bars like me."

"My chin isn't really made from wood," I said.

"Isn't it? That's not what your miniature pig told me and, in fact, he's here now, so take the matter up with him."

And the diver finally rotated his head until I could discern his face in the circular window. Jammed against the glass was a tiny piglet with mischievous eyes who winked at me sardonically.

"But he lives in a jar on a shelf," I protested.

"So you admit he isn't a lie? He outgrew the jar and now lives here, in the helmet of my diving suit. As for the shelf, it was very *shelfish* to keep him there on his own, you rotter. Now he is happier."

I couldn't dispute this. Or rather I could but didn't.

"Right, I've finished. I'll be back here tomorrow at the same hour. In the meantime get them to stop lying, Corker!"

And he clambered up and once again in slow motion he remounted his sled and jerked the reins and the seadogs pulled him away across the seabed and back to the surface of the ocean and thence to land. I hate the way Grillchin has no understanding of the difficulties his agents face in the line of duty. I hate the way he cooks falafels on his lower visage.

Now he was gone I felt vindictive and vengeful.

So I reached out with the mechanical arms and picked up those bones of Jones and tore apart the circle. I didn't make a geometrical shape of my own but carefully fitted the bones together properly.

I thought that if I could reconstruct Jones I would be able to persuade him as a complete skeleton to stop lying. Whole skeletons are more reasonable than individual bones. That was my hypothesis.

Slowly but surely the bones slotted into their correct positions and I tied them in place with lengths of seaweed. The entire process took several hours but finally the skeleton had been reconstructed.

And then I gaped anew. For this man wasn't Jones.

It wasn't a man of any kind.

It was the skeleton of a female. And I knew who.

"Hayley Jude!" I shrieked.

"Hello Pop," she retorted.

"But you don't exist. I made you up."

"Sure you did. And now you made me up for real."

"What shall we do next?"

"Take me with you and I'll be your wife."

"That's against regulations but I think I'll do it anyway. Grillchin will be furious and murderous when he finds out. He'll set the Team on us to tear me apart. I'll have to change my identity."

"Do it. Put on weight and get a job as a policeman and call yourself Cop Porker instead. He'll never know it's you."

It was a good idea. I couldn't open the cockpit to let her in because that would have flooded the interior of the submarine and I would have died, but I picked her up in the mechanical arms and we rose together out of the sea until we reached the air. Then I took her ashore.

My motorised bed was waiting for us. We climbed into it and snuggled up tight. I ordered it to convey us to the residence of Boppo Higgins, for I had been struck by an inspiration. Boppo is such a good inventor that he can invent a device that will extract my skeleton and replace it with Hayley Jude's. Then I will return to the seabed and substitute my own bones for the missing ones. The entire task could be completed in one day.

This way we can trick Grillchin and satisfy all his requirements. He will have a set of bones to use as an artwork and I am confident that my bones won't lie under the sea. In fact that's where I keep my truth, mingled with the marrow inside those white human sticks. It's a good place to keep truth safe. Why not try keeping your own truth there sometime?

Hayley Jude will be inside me until the end of our lives and few couples, no matter how romantic they try to be, can claim this. The fact her skeleton is a bit shorter than my own doesn't matter. My flesh sags on my frame now, but so what? I love Hayley Jude. She's a Corker.

Next time I get a vacation I will take her somewhere nice. I won't use my mishmash ship, nor the submarine, but construct a vessel from slices of charred bread. With luck it will be *tempest toast* on vast waves and go soggy, casting us upon a desert island where we will be safe from detection. Grillchin will be able to fume as much as he likes, to no avail, for he will never find us and, even if he does, we can protest innocence convincingly.

I am sure all will be well or, if not well, then adequate; or, if not adequate, then bearable; or, if not bearable, then vicious.

And, if you believe that, you'll believe anything.

Nonetheless it is true. Isn't it?

Train of Thought

My Train of Thought is leaving from Platform 666 in a few minutes and I haven't even bought a ticket yet.

True, I can purchase one on the train from an inspector but they scowl and hiss when asked, and I am feeling fragile. It has been a hard day and I don't require the hassle. I'm fraught.

Or am I freight? I always get those two mixed up.

It's frightful, friends, believe me!

I recall the good old days, when citizens were allowed to have thoughts at any time they liked, and those thoughts were permitted to go anywhere. It wasn't always wise to voice your thoughts, but the actual thoughts were free. Nobody at all had to pay for them.

And as for timetables, stations, and all that rigmarole...

Perish the thought! Which reminds me:

A Train of Thought did perish yesterday evening. It was in a collision with another Train of Thought coming the other way. The result was bad, a mangled tangle of abstract wreckage.

And, in the middle of all the debris, the bodies of a deep-sea diver and a mountaineer in a close embrace, but whether an embrace of love or hate is tricky to ascertain at this exact instant.

Jack Custard was a diver who loved exploring sunken ships, and he even lived in one for a month, his air being continually replenished by a pump at the surface. The truth is that he hated coming back up. He belonged in the deeps. Downwards was his true home.

He was a very good man and always did kind deeds whenever he had the chance; but he couldn't wait to return to the watery abyss. Diving was his one passion. He was on familiar terms with octopuses, squid, dolphins, and many other kinds of subaquatic beast.

If he could have grown gills, he would have done so...

One day, he was reluctantly riding his bicycle through his

hometown in the direction of the market. He was planning to buy some fruit for supper, but not his own supper: he intended to donate it to some poor people with scurvy who lived next door to him. Students.

As he turned the corner, he was shocked to see another bicycle coming straight at him. There was a collision and—

Witnesses described it in very lurid terms indeed.

But I can't reveal details unless you have a valid ticket. Fatal accidents are a spectator sport these days, that's why.

Hickory Dickory was a mountaineer who loved conquering the highest and hardest peaks, and he even lived on a ledge no wider than a thumb for a month, his food being constantly replenished by a helpful yeti. Upwards was where he belonged. His home was the sky.

He was a nasty man, and always did awful deeds whenever he had the chance, but he couldn't wait to return to the mountaintops. Climbing was his one passion. He was on familiar terms with birds, clouds, balloons, and many other kinds of high altitude inhabitant.

If he could have grown wings, he would have done so…

One day, he was reluctantly riding his bicycle through his hometown in the direction of the market. He was planning to buy a large bottle of olive oil, but not to cook with: he wanted to make his driveway slippery so that any visitors would fall and injure themselves.

As he turned the corner, he was shocked to see another bicycle coming straight at him. There was a collision and—

Witnesses described it in very lurid terms indeed.

But I can't reveal details unless you have a valid ticket. Fatal accidents are a spectator sport these days, that's why.

You already know that, of course. May I see your ticket?

Jack and Hickory blinked at each other.

"You're a ghost!" "So are you!" "The collision killed us!"

"I won't forget this!" "I forgive you!"

Both spirits looked down at their own cadavers, at the ruined bicycles, at the gathering crowd of shocked people.

Then they felt an insistent tugging at their forms.

"I seem to be rising!" cried Jack.

"I seem to be sinking!" Hickory bellowed.

"But I'm a diver. I'm scared of heights. I don't want to go up!"

"I'm a climber. I'm terrified of depths."

"What shall we do then?"

"I don't know. The force is getting stronger…"

The truth is that they were responding to the pull of the afterlife. Jack was being drawn up into Heaven, and Hickory pushed down into Hell. It is ironic that these directions weren't the ones that could ever make them happy. Both Heaven and Hell are fully automated systems and don't care about the phobias we may happen to have.

"If I grab hold of you, and you grab hold of me, and if we cling tight enough to each other then…" ventured Jack.

"…the equal and opposite forces should cancel out," finished Hickory, his eyes burning like soft spherical arsonists.

And so they embraced strongly, arms and legs entwined.

And yes, the forces did balance.

They remained on Earth, which perhaps is how ghosts are born. Mind you, respectable ghosts don't tend to go around in pairs, so forget I said that. I'll delete it before this story is published, unless I'm distracted from doing so by the next unexpected event—

"Jack Custard, you are preventing the soul of a bad man from going to Hell, where it belongs!" boomed the voice of a celestial tannoy. "And that means you are also a bad man. Get down!"

This wasn't an incitement to dance, by the way.

The tannoy voice was automated too, just in case you're wondering. It almost never incited dead people to dance.

"Hickory Dickory, you are stopping a good man's soul from going to Heaven, where it belongs, which is a bad act… and yet that good man is no longer good but bad, so you are preventing a bad man from going to Heaven, which is a good act, which means…"

The logical consequences were simply too confusing.

And that, in fact, was my Train of Thought.

So it has left the station without me. Bloody typical!

I'll tell you something: the new way of doing things isn't

practical and it can't continue like this for much longer.

Bring back the old days. Unrestricted travel for all thoughts!

I'm standing on Platform 666 like a—

Lemon? But that's a cliché. Or is it a cure for scurvy?

The smell of olive oil is in my nostrils.

I can hear the hooves of the students as they clatter along the rails. The teeth in their gums are loose but can still do plenty of damage. I'll use the oil to slow them up. Drizzled on the tracks.

Now *that's* the ticket!

The Haggis Eater

He loved haggis so much, Donald, that he regarded himself as a professional haggis eater, though he received no payment for the act of preparing, consuming and digesting this very peculiar pudding.

And even he, despite his enthusiasm for the product, had to recognise that a haggis really is an odd thing to cook and devour, no argument about it. For, as I'm sure you are aware, it consists of the heart, liver and lungs of a sheep cut up fine with onions, oatmeal, suet and spices.

These ingredients are stuffed into the stomach of the same sheep and then the stomach is simmered in a large pan for three hours or so. In the old days, the hide of the animal would be folded into the shape of a crude cooking vessel and filled with water, then hot stones taken from the camp fire could be lowered into the liquid to bring it to the boil without having to apply a flame directly beneath the hide, which would have damaged it.

But Donald didn't live in the old days now.

Nor had he ever done so.

So he used a pan, a pan as large and deep as a cauldron.

And his cooker was electric.

He was a modern gentlemen but he adored haggis. He worshipped haggis, and his waking and dreaming mind was filled with thoughts of the organic sack of innards that he so ardently wished to transport into his own insides. For most of his life he had been a lover of this food.

Yes, even as a child he had craved haggis, while his friends were far more enamoured with sweet things, and he had often begged his parents for seconds. To his relatives, he became something of a joke but not the kind of joke that mocks, rather, one that is more than half admiration.

"He's a throwback, no doubt," said his father kindly enough to his mother as they watched him attack a third helping.

"Aye, to the days of the clans," his mother said.

"Further back than that," replied his father thoughtfully, "to the era of the wild men who painted their faces blue."

"The Picts," spluttered Donald

"Don't talk with your mouth full," they told him.

"He is asking for a toothpick, is he?" said the grandfather, who always sat in a chair in the corner of the room.

"No, no, he's naming the blue men," said the mother.

"Ah," conceded the grandfather.

But Donald felt no real connection with such distant ancestors. His desire for haggis was unique and had nothing to do with any genetic predisposition he might have been given from long-lost centuries. This could clearly be proved by the fact that his sister loathed the idea of the thing, let along the thing itself, and was sick even when the smell wafted to her nose.

Donald dreamed of becoming a brave haggis hunter when he grew up, for his childish assumption was that a haggis was a creature, something like a living set of bagpipes, with tartan fur. His parents did nothing to correct this idea and it wasn't until he left home that he learned the truth, or rather that the truth learned him, and it happened one night in a restaurant.

"This haggis doesn't taste fresh. When was it caught?" he demanded of a waiter who had served him supper on a plate.

"Caught?" came the baffled reply.

"Aye, that's what I said. Where did it live before it was killed? What hills did it roam and what foods did it eat? I don't think it's a free range one. Could it be the case that this is a battery haggis?"

The waiter responded to the best of his ability but Donald stood in fury to grab the fellow by his shirt and shake him violently, after which he was cast into the street by several other waiters and a chef.

Back in his lodgings, Donald consulted a dictionary.

He felt embarrassed but he also saw the amusing side of his error and his enthusiasm for haggis wasn't diminished at all. If anything it was enhanced, and he decided to learn how to prepare it from scratch, a procedure that required the collusion of a sympathetic butcher; for modern health and safety laws generally prevent experiments with offal by novices.

Yet he found more than one butcher willing to help him for

the sake both of tradition, and as a small act of rebellion against interfering authorities. It took many attempts with the raw ingredients before Donald finally produced a haggis as acceptable as those sold in supermarkets.

His skills rapidly improved and soon he was blending spices to add to the bloody mix of organs to amplify or attenuate, depending on circumstances, the nuttiness and pungency of the end result.

In short: he became an accomplished haggis master.

With a large glass of whisky, two separate small bowls of neeps and tatties, both mashed, he would attack the haggis like a hungry bear disembowels a beehive: with ravenous fury but also care.

In time, he began omitting the turnip and potato.

They were superfluous, he found.

And so was pity for the sheep: he had none. Nor was any expected of him by anyone who knew about his obsession.

He imagined that his present life, culinary and general, would continue in this way forever, or until old age, which to a youth is the same thing. The eating and digesting of haggis would always be his main pastime, his ultimate passion, his reason to *be*. The years would roll, or unable to roll, for they are not in shape spherical, fold themselves behind the present, and yet he would persist, securing the necessary guts and boiling them correctly.

How could anything change?

But Donald won himself a girlfriend, almost accidentally, and something happened – not the kind of something that is just anything, but a highly specific something that only resembles itself.

Her name was Irene and he met her in a part of the story that hasn't been included here, so you will have to imagine it for yourself. They got to like each other more and more and the day soon came when Donald invited her back for a meal at his place. She gladly accepted.

When lovers dine together the bonds of love pull tighter. That's how it is supposed to work, and usually does, but in this instance the outcome wasn't as positive as it might have been. In fact, the evening failed spectacularly, but it can also be said that Donald had no complaints – none at all – and nor does Irene now, for what happened wasn't her fault.

Or perhaps it *was* her fault but the elements of the reaction were already present, and she was merely the catalyst.

Donald opened his front door with his key and led her into the big kitchen and sat her down at a table, and opened a bottle of wine, and lit candles, and other romantic things along similar lines. I'm sure you know what. Then he turned to the cooker and twisted one of the knobs.

"It's been simmering and bubbling all afternoon and now just needs to be warmed up for a wee spell," he announced.

"But what is it?" squinted Irene.

"You'll see," answered Donald with a patrician smile.

"I suppose so," she said.

"There's no 'suppose' about it, young lady."

"Maybe and maybe not."

He supervised the pot and, when it was ready, he drained and emptied it onto a large dish and conveyed the dish to the table. What stood in the centre of that dish almost seemed to throb and Donald beamed, his smugness as perfectly swollen as the revealed haggis itself.

"Presto!" he declared and he parted the veils of steam that rose from the pulsing object and leered across the table at Irene, his head like a speech bubble without any writing inside, just features.

"What is *that*?" shrieked Irene, and the knife and fork she was holding in anticipation dropped out of her limp fingers.

"It's a haggis, my dear!"

"And what exactly does it consist of?"

"Well, it's all the parts of a sheep that would otherwise go to waste, the viscera and the clotted blood, all minced with oats and a few other things like that; also with a particular blend of spices I invented myself, and the mixture then stuffed into the sheep's stomach."

Irene pointed. "You mean to say that this is—"

Donald rubbed his own belly. "A stomach, indeed so. It looks like a full moon that has been distorted by a cosmic disaster of unimaginable magnitude, perhaps a collision with an asteroid. It glows an unhealthy yellow and yet I say it's the finest culinary delight ever!"

"I have no stomach for it," said Irene.

Donald giggled at what he assumed was a joke. "Tuck in, my dear, don't be shy. I prepared it especially for you."

"I wish you hadn't," said Irene.

"Then it's your lucky day, for the truth is that I prepared it especially for me, but with you in mind also, which proves that wishes *can* come true at least sometimes. But let's start eating it!"

"I am going to decline that pleasure, if it's all the same to you. I think I'll limit myself to drinking this wine."

"Are you mad? Are you a lunatic, my dear?"

Donald was sincerely mortified.

But Irene remained firm in her refusal and he was forced to serve the first portion to himself alone, and eat it without any feeling this was a communal act; a feast of togetherness, a bonding ritual.

Irene observed him as he worked his way through the monstrosity, and it was two thirds finished before she asked:

"How many of these things have you devoured?"

"Hundreds," he said, mouth full.

"But they are *stomachs*. A stomach digests food. How can you be sure it isn't digesting you from the inside?"

"Don't be silly. My teeth mash it up into tiny pieces. Even if I could open my jaw wide enough to swallow a haggis whole, it would be a stomach within a stomach and the inner stomach would merely digest its own contents rather than what lay around it. After all, our own stomachs don't digest our hearts, kidneys and livers, do they? We remain intact!"

"But you just admitted that your teeth cut it up into bits. What if these bits reassemble themselves into a stomach inside you, not the way a stomach is, but as an *inside-out* stomach? Then it would certainly digest you and there wouldn't be anything much you could do about it."

"The odds against that happening," he roared pompously, "are more than a thousand million billion trillion to one."

"So it's not impossible?" persisted Irene.

He was about to answer but something prevented him. What was it? Irene realised he was shrinking. Not only shrinking, but dissolving too. It was the look on her face, astonishment mixed with triumph, that stopped him saying what he intended to say. Now he felt himself growing tenuous, becoming thinner, and less of a man; his flesh turning to liquid, and this liquid vanishing as his essence was absorbed by the inside-out stomach.

He was all gone. On the chair in his place sat a haggis.

Belated Foreword

The very idea of the 'foreword' is a peculiar one. Books have them, yes, but why not trains, ducks, slippers, balconies, harpsichords, bloated lips, or cashew nuts? I would happily write a foreword to a strawberry tart. Why haven't I done so? It's a mystery. No matter. The world is full of mysteries, and so much the better for it! A century ago, lived a writer by the name of Abraham Merritt. He was quite famous for some years and many other authors hugely praised his merits. Now he is obscure. Time did that to him. I'm glad I don't have to shoulder the blame!

Merritt wrote books with beautiful titles, evocative titles that suggest a deeper sense of mystery and wonder than the actual works can possibly deliver. Perhaps he did his best to match content to subtle promise, perhaps not, I don't know. But it still seems to me that his *Dwellers in the Mirage* is one of the finest titles ever conceived; a title so superb I always wanted it for my own. I couldn't steal it unaltered, of course, but I've finally managed to assuage my envy by adapting it to my own needs. Hence *Mirrors in the Deluge*, a curiously Welsh reversal, I feel!

Elsewhen Press
an independent publisher specialising in Speculative Fiction

Visit the Elsewhen Press website at elsewhen.press for the latest information on all of our titles, authors and events; to read our blog; find out where to buy our books and ebooks; or to place an order.

Elsewhen Press

an independent publisher specialising in Speculative Fiction

THE RHYMER
an Heredyssey

DOUGLAS THOMPSON

"Simply Stupendous" – Rhys Hughes

The Rhymer, an Heredyssey defies classification in any one literary genre. A satire on contemporary society, particularly the art world, it is also a comic-poetic meditation on the nature of life, death and morality.

A mysterious tramp wanders from town to town, taking a new name and identity from whoever he encounters first. Apparently amnesiac or even brain-damaged, Nadith Learmot nonetheless has other means to access the past and perhaps even the future: upon his chest a dial, down his sleeves wires that he can connect to the walls of old buildings from which he believes he can read their ghosts like imprints on tape. Haunting him constantly is the resemblance he apparently bears to his supposed brother, a successful artist called Zenir. Setting out to pursue Zenir and denounce or blackmail him out of spite, in his travels around the satellite towns and suburbs surrounding a city called Urbis, Nadith finds he is always two steps behind a figure as enigmatic and polyfaceted as himself. But through second hand snippets of news he increasingly learns of how his brother's fortunes are waning, while his own, to his surprise, are on the rise. Along the way, he encounters unexpected clues to his own true identity, how he came to lose his memory and acquire his strange 'contraption'. When Nadith finally catches up with Zenir, what will they make of each other?

Told entirely in the first person in a rhythmic stream of lyricism, Nadith's story reads like Shakespeare on acid, leaving the reader to guess at the truth that lies behind his madness. Is Nadith a mental health patient or a conman? ... Or as he himself comes to believe, the reincarnation of the thirteenth century Scottish seer True Thomas The Rhymer, a man who never lied nor died but disappeared one day to return to the realm of the faeries who had first given him his clairvoyant gifts?

Douglas Thompson's short stories have appeared in a wide range of magazines and anthologies. He won the Grolsch/Herald Question of Style Award in 1989 and second prize in the Neil Gunn Writing Competition in 2007. His first book, *Ultrameta*, published in 2009, was nominated for the Edge Hill Prize, and shortlisted for the BFS Best Newcomer Award. Since then he has published more novels, including *Entanglement* published by Elsewhen Press. *The Rhymer* is his eighth novel.

ISBN: 9781908168511 (epub, kindle)
ISBN: 9781908168412 (192pp paperback)
Visit bit.ly/TheRhymer-Heredyssey

Elsewhen Press

an independent publisher specialising in Speculative Fiction

A series of novels attempting to document the trials and tribulations of the **Transdimensional Authority**

Ira Nayman

If there were Alternate Realities, and in each there was a version of Earth (very similar, but perhaps significantly different in one particular regard, or divergent since one particular point in history) then imagine the problems that could be caused if someone, somewhere, managed to work out how to travel between them. Those problems would be ideal fodder for a News Service that could also span all the realities. Now you understand the reasoning behind the Alternate Reality News Service (ARNS). But you aren't the first. In fact, Canadian satirist and author Ira Nayman got there before you and has been the conduit for ARNS into our Reality for some years now, thanks to his website *Les Pages aux Folles*.

But also consider that if there were problems being caused by unregulated travel between realities, it's not just news but a perfect ~~excuse~~ reason to establish an Authority to oversee such travel and make sure that it is regulated. You probably thought jurisdictional issues are bad enough between competing national agencies of dubious acronym and even more dubious motivation, let alone between agencies from different nations. So imagine how each of them would cope with an Authority that has jurisdiction across the realities in different dimensions. Now, you understand the challenges for the investigators who work for the Transdimensional Authority (TA). But, perhaps more importantly, you can see the potential for humour. Again, Ira beat you to it.

Ira Nayman is the creator of *Les Pages aux Folles*, a Web site of political and social satire that is over 10 years old (that's positively Paleolithic in Internet years!). Five collections of Alternate Reality News Service (ARNS) stories which originally appeared on the Web site have been self-published in print. Ira's Web Goddess tells him he should make more of the fact that he won the 2010 Jonathan Swift Satire Writing Contest. So, Ira won the 2010 Jonathan Swift Satire Writing Contest.

Welcome to the Multiverse[*]

[*] Sorry for the inconvenience

Being the first

ISBN: 9781908168191 (epub, kindle)

ISBN: 9781908168092 (336pp paperback)

You Can't Kill the Multiverse[*]

[*] But You Can Mess With its Head

Being the second

ISBN: 9781908168399 (epub, kindle)

ISBN: 9781908168290 (320pp paperback)

Random Dingoes

Being the third

ISBN: 9781908168795 (epub, kindle)

ISBN: 9781908168696 (288pp paperback)

Visit bit.ly/TransdimensionalAuthority

Elsewhen Press

an independent publisher specialising in Speculative Fiction

DANDELION TRILOGY
MIKE FRENCH

Literary surrealism, contemporary fantasy, biting satire, dystopian science fiction. The Dandelion Trilogy by Mike French is all of these and more. Starting with *The Ascent of Isaac Steward*, this is literary surrealism at its most profound. A contemporary fantasy that follows one man's journey into his own mind as he struggles to come to terms with the trauma that has reshaped his life and starts to question his own existence. Moving forward to 2034 in *Blue Friday*, this biting satire warns of a Britain where overtime for married couples is banned, there is enforced viewing of family television (much of it repeats of old shows from the sixties and seventies), monitored family meal-times and a coming of age where twenty-five year-olds are automatically assigned a spouse by the state computer if they have failed to marry. Only the Overtime Underground network resists with the illicit Avodah drug to increase productivity. Finally *Convergence* delivers us into a truly dystopian future, where a covert military/governmental project uses prisoners on death row to explore what happens to people as they die, downloading the Convergence Point formed in the brain's memory at the point of death into clones. But when combined with Avodah they inadvertently trigger what may be the end of humanity – or a new beginning.

What does it have to do with dandelions? You'll have to read it to find out...

Mike French is the owner and senior editor of the prestigious literary magazine, *The View From Here*. Mike's debut novel, *The Ascent of Isaac Steward* was published in 2011 and nominated for The Galaxy National Book Awards. He currently lives in Luton with his wife, three children and a growing number of pets.

Book 1: The Ascent of Isaac Steward
ISBN: 9781908168351 (epub, kindle)
ISBN: 9781908168252 (224pp paperback)

Book 2: Blue Friday
ISBN: 9781908168177 (epub, kindle)
ISBN: 9781908168078 (192pp paperback)

Book 3: Convergence
ISBN: 9781908168368 (epub, kindle)
ISBN: 9781908168269 (256pp paperback)

Visit bit.ly/DandelionTrilogy

About the author

Rhys Hughes was born in 1966 and began writing from an early age. His first short story was published in 1991 and his first book, the now legendary *Worming the Harpy*, followed four years later. Since then he has published more than thirty books, his work has been translated into ten languages and he is currently one of the most prolific and successful authors in Wales. *Mirrors in the Deluge* is the first of his books to be published by Elsewhen Press.

Mostly known for absurdist works, his range in fact encompasses styles as diverse as gothic, experimental, science fiction, magic realism, fantasy and realism. His main ambition is to complete a grand sequence of exactly one thousand linked short stories, a project he has been working on for more than two decades. Each story is a standalone piece as well as a cog in the grand machine. He is finally three-quarters of the way through this opus.